SHADOW BITTEN

SHADOW CITY: ROYAL VAMPIRE

JEN L. GREY

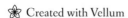

CHAPTER ONE

I wasn't sure which was worse, the way Annie, my foster sister and best friend, had her arm wrapped around me to keep me in place, or the knife she was pressing to my neck.

Blood dripped onto my lap and drizzled on the maroon rug in the middle of the all-concrete basement hidden beneath Shadow Terrace's blood bank. My injured neck screamed from being wrenched in the same position for so long. The brown loveseat beside us had been tossed onto its side during the scuffle between me and Zaro, one of the vampires who'd brought me here.

My head grew woozy from the lack of oxygen and blood loss. My vision hazed. The jagged edge of the knife dug deeper into my skin, a mixed blessing. It hurt, but the sharp pain kept me grounded.

Her words—*this is what you deserve, bitch*—echoed in my head, solidifying the sickening realization that Eilam, a vampire who lacked virtually all his humanity, had messed with Annie's mind, turning her into someone I didn't recognize.

The shadow that had haunted and petrified me since childhood rushed toward me. It had helped me kill Zaro, but I hadn't asked for its help now. No matter how hard it was not to blame Annie, I didn't want anything to happen to my sister, but somehow, the shadow always showed up when I was most vulnerable, physically, and emotionally.

A howl bit through the basement. My wolf shifter friends had found the hidden door to the room where I was being held captive. The wolves' excited baying was followed by a loud thump and a crack as the doorway to the blood bank splintered.

Veronica! Alex used our soulmate connection to speak to me telepathically. *Talk to me. You can't say I love you like that and then go silent.* His terror slammed into me, and my emotions damn near overwhelmed me.

"Why are you hesitating?" Eilam hissed, forcing my attention to him. "Bring her to me." He straddled Gwen, Alex's sister and Shadow Terrace's vampire princess, holding her wrists. His long, jet-black hair had fallen from his low ponytail and hung in his face, contrasting against his ivory skin. His ice-blue eyes, outlined with crimson, glared with disdain at Annie and me.

"I ...I can't." Annie's soft voice broke, but she didn't force me closer to him. Hope sprang inside me. Maybe her real self was trying to break free.

"This won't be over that easily," he snarled and

released Gwen's wrist, only to punch her in the face again.

Her head jerked to the side, and Eilam fisted her ivory hair and dragged her toward me. The beautiful vampire wasn't recognizable with her face covered in blood. Her nose was bent unnaturally. Not even her chestnut eyes were visible through the swelling.

With each step he took, her dingy white crop top inched higher, revealing a white lace bra underneath. Gwen twisted, trying to get free of his hold, but she was too weak. She managed to grab his arm, but her hands soon fell away.

"Cut her more," Eilam growled at Annie.

Gwen whimpered, "I don't want to feed from her."

"You'll change your mind once you start," Eilam promised, pulling her closer to me.

Annie's hand shook as she tightened her hold.

The shadow reached its hand toward me, and I recoiled with fear.

"No." I couldn't let it hurt Annie.

It retreated into the corner, surprising me. It had *listened*?

"You don't have to do this." The knife dug deeper with each word I said, but I had to reach her. "It's not too late. The strong girl I love is somewhere inside you."

Her hand shook. I could tell some sort of internal struggle was going on.

"Don't listen to her," Eilam warned. "You belong to me. She's trying to come between us."

"You know that's not true." Even if I couldn't get

through to her completely, if I could buy more time, the others would be here momentarily. *How damn close are you?*

We're breaking through now, Alex growled as another loud crack shook the walls.

"No!" Eilam yelled and kicked Gwen in the stomach. She flew the rest of the way to me.

She covered her nose with her hand and rocked back and forth, her body shaking. I wasn't sure if she trembled from fighting the urge to attack me or from all the pain. From the way Eilam was acting, I'd bank on the first option.

Eilam blurred to Gwen and clutched her head. He lifted it and brought it close to my neck. I tried to jerk back, but Annie still held me tight.

"Annie, please," I pleaded, voice cracking.

The sound of paws hitting the ground comforted me. They padded closer, but that didn't mean I'd make it out of here alive.

Gwen's teeth extended, and she grimaced with disgust. She pushed back against Eilam to put distance between us.

"She's not bleeding enough," Eilam said. "Fuck it. Kill her."

My heart dropped.

This was it.

At least, I'd gotten a moment of happiness with Alex before my life ended.

"I...I can't." Annie dropped the knife and released me. I crumpled into a fetal position. "I'm sorry." She stumbled back and leaned against the wall. Some of her wavy, brown-sugar hair stuck to the blood-soaked collar of her violet shirt, and her red lipstick was smudged around her mouth. She didn't appear well.

I wasn't sure if she was talking to Eilam or me, but I didn't give a damn. My sister was strong enough to fight whatever manipulation he had over her.

The *yank*ing took root deep in my chest as a figure blurred toward me. Even though I couldn't make out his features, the connection between Alex and me was unmistakable. My heart almost burst with joy that I would get to see him one more time.

As he materialized in front of me, black wings whooshed past me. Rosemary lifted Eilam off the floor, forcing him to release Gwen, and rammed him into the concrete wall. Groaning, he slid down the wall and into a heap. Rosemary loomed over him, ready to strike.

"Oh, God." Gwen scrambled off the floor and staggered to the far corner where she'd been chained. Blood still glistened on the spiked cuffs that had bound her wrists. She inhaled through her mouth as if she couldn't stand to breathe through her nose. The smell of my blood had to be getting to her.

Alex hovered in front of me, his six-foot frame shielding me from Annie, and hissed. His body tensed, and his hands clenched at his sides as he stared my sister down. Able to feel my pain, he looked broken.

"Hey." Despite my body screaming in pain, I stood and touched his shoulder, needing him to focus on me and not my sister. "She let me go before you got here."

"We can't trust her." He glanced over his shoulder at me, his fangs descended, and his soft blue eyes focused on my neck wound. "This could be a ploy."

Needing more of his touch, I wrapped my arms around him. The sweet syrup scent that was uniquely his filled my nose. It was my favorite smell in the entire world. "No, he wanted her to kill me. He commanded it."

A silver wolf ran into the room. Sterlyn was twice the size of the other wolves, but that didn't faze them. Killian's dark espresso wolf and Griffin's sandy-blond wolf flanked her on either side. The three of them circled me, protecting me from Eilam and Gwen. Sierra's dirty-blond wolf trotted over and sat at my feet, staring down at Annie. I had no doubt they had become my true friends; these people had more than proved their loyalty to me.

"And she did that to you." Alex lifted my head, his face contorting in agony when he saw my wound. Anger rolled off him.

"Let me explain." Eilam lifted his hands. "This is all a misunderstanding."

Wow. For once, I was speechless. Did he actually think that would work?

"Oh, do tell." Rosemary smirked and tilted her head, letting her mahogany hair cascade down her back. She relaxed her wings, and the feathers blended in with her black shirt. "I'd love to hear how escaping jail, black-mailing Ronnie to come here, sneaking her through an underground tunnel into a hidden room that no one knew about, and trying to get the vampire princess to feed off her was all a misunderstanding."

"Obviously, Alex cares about her." Eilam lifted a hand at me and winced. "If the vampire prince is emotionally invested in a human, shouldn't we make sure she has the ability to integrate into our world?"

"You did this for me?" Alex said sincerely, pivoting to face the idiot.

Sierra countered Alex's move by positioning herself in front of me. She eyed Annie, who was panting against the wall. My sister touched the bite marks on her neck that marked where Eilam had fed off her.

"Yes." Eilam stood slowly.

Rosemary didn't move an inch, but her twilight eyes watched the vampire's every move.

A faint grin spread across Eilam's face. He thought Alex *believed* him. "Anything for my prince. You know all of us vampires are devoted to the royal family."

"Then what about Annie?" Keeping my mouth shut would've been the smart thing to do, but I couldn't. "You aren't supposed to feed from a human and control her mind, but you did. Was that for your prince too?"

"You may have captured Prince Alex's attention," Eilam sneered, "but you are just a human, and I don't answer to you."

"That's not true." Alex wrapped his arm around my waist and glared at the vampire. "You do answer to her. She is, after all, my soulmate, and we've completed our bond."

Realization settled over Eilam, and the cocky sneer fell from his face. He inhaled sharply. "That's impossible."

"Why do you think I told Veronica where we were located as soon as she got here? We made sure we brought backup too." Gwen rasped from the corner of the room.

She was in worse shape than me, and that was saying something. I'd seen everything she'd gone through since I'd gotten here—and I could only imagine what I'd missed.

Alex pulled me against his side. *She's showing her support for our relationship, so he doesn't think there are any inner-family issues.*

But I had a feeling it was more than that. *And that she's fine with Rosemary and the wolves trespassing in Shadow Terrace too?*

They might have something to do with it, Alex admitted, his honesty warming my heart. We'd come a long way in such a short time.

"That's how you found us." Eilam's eyes widened, and he shook his head. "But she's human. How can she have a supernatural link?"

"No one knows, but that's not the concern." Alex released me and picked up the knife that Annie had dropped. "I want to know who supports you in this initiative and how long it's been going on."

"I'd rather die than tell you." Eilam chuckled as if he knew something no one else did. "And here I thought this would get us all on the same page, but instead, you are mated to a human. The royal family isn't as strong as it once was. When everyone finds out the truth, they'll turn against you."

It had never crossed my mind that my bond with Alex could cause problems for him. He'd always been worried about the target on my back, not his. *Is this true?*

It doesn't matter. He ran a hand through his sun-kissed brown hair. *You're mine, and there's no changing that,* he said possessively.

And dammit, I liked it. A whole damn lot. *I don't want to cause problems—*

They'll learn to live with it, whether they like it or not. Alex stepped in front of me. "They won't turn against me because I'll kill every last person who gets in my way."

"You've never killed anyone." Eilam chuckled. "Matthew and Gwen have always done the dirty work. You're the laughingstock of the entire clan."

"You're mistaken." Alex lifted his chin and peered down his nose at the vampire. "I killed Klyn, and I'll kill anyone else who threatens my mate or my family."

Eilam laughed. "You're full of—"

In a blur of movement, Alex was standing next to Rosemary, stabbing Eilam in the heart. Alex gripped the knife buried in the vampire's chest and stared him in the eyes. "I figure actions speak louder than words," he snarled.

"You...will..." Blood bubbled from Eilam's mouth, and his alabaster skin grew even paler. Gasping for air, he fell to the floor. A trail of blood stained the wall. "... pay."

Silence descended as our group watched his breathing become shallower.

Terror seized my heart. *We have to get him to let Annie go before he dies.*

She'll be fine once he's dead, Alex reassured me. *I'll clear everything up once his influence has vanished.*

Good. The bastard couldn't die fast enough, but he deserved a slow and painful death.

"Alex," Gwen gritted out, clawing her injured face. "Blood—now. I can't wait much longer."

That was enough to snap my mate back to reality. "Give me a minute. I'll get some now." He disappeared from the room.

Rosemary kept her focus on Eilam, watching as the life drained out of him, while Sterlyn and the wolves turned to Gwen. The vampire's fangs were digging into her bottom lip. Her breathing turned labored, and a red hue filled her irises. Her teeth grew even longer, and she hissed, "Hurry, dammit."

She fisted her hands so hard that her jagged nails cut into her skin, and blood dripped from her palms. Her gaze latched onto my neck where blood had stopped dripping.

A strangled cry ripped from her throat as she stood and staggered toward me.

Growling, Griffin charged at the vampire and attempted to take out her legs, but he'd underestimated her desire for my blood. Fueled by her bloodlust, she easily jumped over him.

A faint chuckle left Eilam. He was still alive. "I knew this wasn't over," he said, barely above a whisper.

Gwen blurred, charging right at me.

CHAPTER TWO

My heartbeat picked up as the shadow appeared beside me. I didn't know what to do. I didn't want to hurt Gwen, but I had to fend her off.

The shadow moved, blocking me, but that made no sense. When I was a kid, it had tormented me. No one else could see it, meaning Gwen had no clue it was here.

Time slowed as Rosemary flew toward me and Sterlyn charged at the fast-moving girl. Injured, Gwen wasn't moving at her fastest, and the silver wolf collided with her. The princess dropped to the floor. Sterlyn stood over her, baring her teeth at the vampire.

"Stand behind me," Rosemary commanded, moving in front of me and the shadow. "She isn't in her right mind."

"Annie!" I glanced over my shoulder at my sister, now sitting on the floor, clutching her head.

"Sierra, guard Annie." Rosemary stiffened, her focus

on Gwen as Griffin and Killian closed in around the vampire beside Sterlyn.

The dirty-blond wolf obeyed and ran to my sister. Once she reached her, some of my anxiety drifted away, but not enough. From what they'd told me, Sierra wasn't the best fighter among them. "Maybe you should protect her too."

"You're more at risk because of your wounds." Rosemary lowered her head like she was about to steamroll Gwen. "You're the one she's after."

I exhaled for what felt like the first time since I'd entered this room. At least, Annie wasn't on Gwen's radar, and I had both Rosemary and the shadow protecting me. Granted, the shadow might kill her. Even though it had protected me, it still held a sinister edge that rocked me to my core.

Hissing, Gwen tried to get to her feet, but Sterlyn head-butted her, knocking her back to the floor. Sterlyn could have done much worse, but she was striking her in ways that wouldn't further hurt the injured vampire.

"Get out of my way, dog," Gwen growled and swiped at Sterlyn. "If I don't eat, I'll die."

So that was what Eilam had done. He'd forced her to choose between her life and mine. Of course, her survival instincts had kicked in, desperation taking root.

Where the hell are you? We needed Alex back here quickly.

On my way back. Alex sounded tense, reflecting the emotion in the room. *I needed to find the freshest blood. It will heal her the fastest.*

I wasn't sure if I was annoyed or relieved that he'd taken the time to do that. *She's attacking, so please hurry up.*

Whatever they do, don't let Rosemary or the wolves hurt Gwen unless your life is at stake, Alex said with trepidation. *If they injure her further, it'll make the situation worse.*

I bit my tongue to keep my thoughts from spilling out. He had to be insinuating that the king—his brother—would be upset that the wolves and the angel had breached their sacred barrier, which was complete bullshit. Matthew already despised that Alex had stayed with me at Sterlyn's house. This would give him more ammunition against Alex. But complaining about it would only add more drama to an already theatrical situation. Our focus needed to stay on feeding Gwen.

"Gwen, hold on." Drawing her attention to me when she was already desperate for my blood wasn't smart, but I hoped my words would diffuse the situation. "Alex is almost back. He found you fresh blood so you can heal quickly."

"I can't wait any longer." The pain in her voice nearly broke me. "I'm slipping away," she said, attempting to stand again.

"Stay quiet," Rosemary barked, her eyes shooting daggers at me over her shoulder. "You're making things worse."

Sterlyn placed her paws on Gwen's shoulders, forcing the vampire back down, and pinned her to the floor. Killian and Griffin each lay on one of Gwen's arms and legs to keep her stationary.

Gwen thrashed, and Sterlyn's nails dug into her skin through her shirt. Blood soaked through the fabric, and Sterlyn whined.

We couldn't afford for Gwen to lose more blood, but if we didn't detain her, she'd kill me.

Something hit the door as the *yank* inside me intensified.

Alex was here.

His figure blurred past me to his sister. He dropped to his knees beside her with a dozen blood bags in his arms, tossing all but one on the floor. He ripped open its line and put the plastic tube in her mouth.

Gwen pulled from it immediately, and half the bag vanished within seconds.

"Let her up," Alex told the wolves. He dropped the empty blood bag, ripped open another one, then placed it in his sister's mouth.

She sat up and grabbed the bag, draining the contents within seconds. She and Alex continued the process, and with each bag drained, her face and body returned to normal.

An ear-shattering scream projected from Annie. Her fingers dug into her forehead, and blood trickled into her eyes. I raced to her, ignoring Sierra's growl as I approached. She didn't want me near Annie after all the shit she'd pulled today, but my sister was in pain.

"Eilam just died," Rosemary said, rushing to my side.

"Okay?" I asked, unsure what that meant. All I

knew was that my friend was screaming in agony and hurting herself. I snagged her hands and forced them away from her face so she couldn't scratch herself anymore.

The amount of pain reflected in her expression fractured me inside. I'd seen Annie like this only once before, two years ago when the neighborhood dog that would visit our house every day had gotten hit by a car. She was always so happy and strong that seeing her fall apart made me break along with her.

A hand touched my shoulder, and the *yank* grew even stronger as I dropped Annie's hands. Warmth spread through my body. Alex said, "It's the mind control. It's unraveling now that he's dead. We'd hoped he would undo it himself so she wouldn't have to go through this, but he had no intention of releasing her."

"Why is it painful?" I hated that I couldn't help her.

"She can remember everything." Alex stepped up beside me. "I'm sorry I couldn't get to Annie in time, but Gwen needed my help."

"There's nothing to be sorry about." He couldn't possibly believe that I blamed him, that he even considered I could hold him at fault. "You were taking care of your sister, who protected me and Annie, and you killed Eilam." I cupped his cheek and kissed his lips lightly. "You made the right choice."

"Ronnie?" Annie sobbed softly, her voice hoarse from screaming.

I dropped my hand and spun around to my sister.

She scanned the room, and her face turned pale.

"Where are we? Is this a dream?" She clutched my arm. "Please, wake me up."

"What?" Glancing at the room, I saw everything she was taking in.

A gorgeous woman with gigantic black wings sprouting from her back.

Four wolves standing inside an underground room, acting like domestic house dogs.

Two dead vampires that had been stabbed in the heart.

And a woman with large fangs and blood-red eyes, draining a blood bag with eight empty ones around her, her face smoothing back into her normal complexion.

In other words, nothing that would make sense to a human and something that would've made me think I'd gone crazy not even two weeks ago.

Now, this all seemed normal to me. So much had changed that I didn't recognize myself.

Please, make her forget everything. I didn't want my new normal to be hers. She deserved a human life, not the craziness that had become mine.

Alex squatted beside her. *Are you sure?*

Yes. The word was thick with emotion at what the decision meant. Mine and Annie's relationship would be changed forever. She would head back home to decide which college to attend, none of which would be Shadow Ridge University, and I would stay here by Alex's side. There was no way I could leave him, or the others, not after everything we'd been through. *She isn't safe here.*

Neither are you. Alex leaned forward. "Annie, everything is going to be okay."

If you're trying to get rid of me, it won't work. Even if I'd wanted to leave, I couldn't. My heart belonged to him. Not being with Annie and Eliza every day would hurt, but it didn't compare to what it would be like to lose Alex. *I'm here. We both know that decision was made the night we cemented our bond.*

I hate the selfish part of me that loves hearing that. He frowned, but his voice didn't lose its soft edge. "Do you want me to make your head better?" he asked Annie. *I want her permission first, though.*

What if she doesn't give it? I didn't want her to make a decision she'd regret later in life.

Her mind is revolting. Alex sighed. *She'll say yes.*

Proving him right, Annie bobbed her head. "Yes. Just make everything make sense again. My head hurts so damn bad."

"Okay." He placed a finger under her chin.

A low growl rattled my chest, surprising me, and he dropped his hand. Jealousy had overwhelmed me from him innocently touching my sister. Something had to be wrong with me.

"Hey." Rosemary snapped her fingers in front of my face, breaking me from my stupor. "Get your shit together. I know you're human and mated to a vampire..." She stopped like she had to process what she'd just said. She blinked and then continued like she hadn't paused at all. "He's not doing anything to upset you. Even though I don't like what he's doing, keeping our kind secret is important, so let your mate do this."

She was right. I had to control myself. He was doing what I'd asked him to do, for goodness' sake. "You're right. Locking it down."

Are you good? Alex arched an eyebrow as an arrogant grin crossed his face.

The asshole enjoyed seeing me jealous. *Yeah, I'll manage.* I'd almost lied but caught myself, knowing I'd stink up the entire room if I did.

His eyes glowed, turning soft blue as he leaned over, catching Annie's attention. "Once you leave, you will forget everything strange and horrible about your time here. Until then, this is all normal and you aren't afraid. Once you leave this town, you'll only remember visiting your boyfriend, who acted in a jealous rage. You tried to work it out, but you realized you don't need that in your life. During this horrible time, Veronica met an amazing guy who treats her well. That would be me."

"And here I thought Sierra was bad," Rosemary groaned. "I think I found someone more arrogant than her."

Sierra's wolf head snapped to Rosemary, and she huffed.

Tell them to quiet down before they mess up my memory molding. He snickered, his amusement flowing through the connection. *They need to leave the insults for when I can listen and fully appreciate them.*

Yeah, I wasn't telling them the last part. I whispered, knowing they could all hear me, "He says to be quiet."

"I'm sure the vampire prince is enjoying ordering us around," Rosemary grumbled but went silent.

"You'll tell—" He cut off. *Who is she going home to?*

Eliza. My heart hurt. I had to figure out what to tell my foster mom, but that was a problem for another day. *She needs to go home and tell her I stayed behind to spend more time with you.* I didn't want to lie to anyone, but I wasn't ready to tell them that I wasn't coming back. Hurt tugged at my heart, but it would hurt worse to leave Alex behind. And it wasn't like Alex could move to Lexington. This was his home and where we were meant to be.

"You'll tell Eliza that Veronica stayed behind with me," he said simply. "We'll come by soon to visit so she can meet me."

Okay, I hadn't expected that.

"I want to stay here with Ronnie," Annie said and tried to tear her gaze from his.

He moved his head, maintaining their connection. "Like I said, we'll come visit you soon, but Veronica needs to stay here while we figure things out."

She nodded slowly. "I want to leave." She shivered. "Can someone please take me to my car?"

Shit, I hadn't even thought about the car.

Alex glanced at Rosemary, then at the wolves. "Why don't you take her to the pack neighborhood? That way you won't be here when Matthew arrives. He's inevitably on his way. I'll bring Annie's car to you."

That sounded like a good plan. "You can leave through the tunnel." I pointed to the back of the room where the vampires had dragged me inside. "It'll let you out near the town border and by my car."

I pulled out the car key and tossed it to Rosemary as I hurried over to Zaro's body. I dug into his pocket and pulled out the key to the angel-proof gate that had prevented Rosemary from following us here. The metal was cool to the touch from Zaro's unnaturally cool body. "And here is this key to the gate."

"Good idea." Rosemary waved at the wolves.

Shouts came from the blood bank above.

"Matthew is here." Alex gestured to the door. "You all go. Veronica, go with them."

Oh, hell no. "I'm staying with you."

"Please, you don't need to be here for this." Alex kissed me. "He's angry, and it's best if you aren't around."

The image of that day in the bar flashed in my mind. Matthew was the one who'd clued me in that something strange was going on in this town.

Rosemary picked up Annie and cradled her as she flew out the door toward the underground tunnel with the four wolves trailing behind her. Sterlyn stopped and glanced back at me.

I shook my head. "I'm staying."

She nodded and caught up with the others.

"Veronica..." Alex warned, but it was too late.

Matthew bellowed from outside the broken door, "What the fuck is going on?"

CHAPTER THREE

Y*ou should've gone with them.* Alex grabbed my arm and tugged me slightly behind him.

Nope. That wasn't happening. We were in this together. *When we completed our connection, you were agreeing to have me by your side just as much as I was agreeing to be part of this world. How will your brother ever accept me if you treat me like I'm not meant to be here?*

Alex's shoulders sagged. *That's the thing. I was being selfish by completing the connection with you. I should've let you go, but I couldn't.*

His words stung even though he hadn't meant them to. The hurt wafted off me, and his expression crumpled as Matthew entered the room.

"I asked a question." Matthew surveyed the room, searching for something.

If I had to guess, it'd be four wolves and an angel.

"Well, let's see, *brother*." After finishing the last blood bag, Gwen mostly appeared like her normal self. When she stood, she swayed a little, revealing she wasn't fully recovered. "I got captured in Eilam's house and tortured. But thanks for checking on me first."

"You look fine, Gwen," Matthew said, his dark gaze landing on me. "Why the hell is she here and not that stupid girl we were protecting?"

"Eilam blackmailed Veronica into meeting with him and used an underground tunnel system to bring her here." Alex straightened his shoulders. "And that's not why you're so angry. Say what's really on your mind."

"Fine." Matthew marched deeper into the room and sniffed. "Their scents are still heavy in the air. So where the hell are they? I didn't see them leave."

Between Alex hurting me and Matthew being an asshole, I couldn't hide my animosity. "Here's an idea. Maybe they used the same hidden tunnel as the vampires."

Please, don't attract more attention to yourself, Alex pleaded, pissing me off even more.

Matthew's eyes focused on me, turning crimson, but his fangs hadn't appeared. Not yet. "You do realize you're human and it wouldn't take much to snap that pretty little neck of yours."

"And you do realize," Alex rasped as he moved in front of me, "I've killed two other vampires who've threatened my *mate*."

A little bit of my anger thawed. A little bit. He was protecting me, but he'd still acted like a jerk.

"I'm your brother and king." Matthew cracked his neck as if to intimidate Alex. "You wouldn't be so foolish."

"Are you sure about that?" Alex stood taller. "I respect you, but I can't live without her."

"Another questionable decision you've made." Matthew grimaced and gestured to Eilam. "Along with killing him. I almost don't recognize the man standing in front of me anymore."

Wow. I hadn't realized such a big rift existed between these two. I sort of felt bad since I seemed partly to blame.

"He was in jail for weeks with no blood." Alex's hands fisted, and his body tensed. "And he somehow broke out and kidnapped his *princess* and his blood whor—" Alex paused and inhaled sharply. "Slave. And his blood slave."

Shock coursed through me, and it took a second for what he'd been about to call her to sink in. *Were you about to call my sister a whore?*

Out of habit. He at least had the decency to sound ashamed. "Not to mention," Alex continued, speaking to Matthew, "he blackmailed my *mate* into coming here to make Gwen kill her. Please, tell me why I shouldn't have killed him?"

"Because we now have nothing to go on." Matthew threw his hands out to his sides. "What's our next step in figuring out who's part of the rogue vampires? Not to mention you involved outsiders in our problem. You've escalated the situation by putting your *human* mate ahead of the good of your people."

"Matthew, I understand where you're coming from." Gwen rubbed her healed, blood-crusted wrists.

"See!" Matthew marched over to Gwen. "Gwen agrees with me like you should—"

"Let me finish," Gwen snapped.

I had to hold back my laughter because I enjoyed seeing her put the cocky asshole in his place.

Matthew turned to her and nodded smugly. "Sure. Sorry. Please proceed."

"As I was saying before I was rudely interrupted..." Gwen glared. "I don't think you're right."

"What?" His brow furrowed. "Are you agreeing with *him?*

"Look, Annie came here of her own accord. Veronica had nothing to do with her being here. If anyone is to blame, it's either Eilam and his partners or the university for allowing humans to visit. Maybe a combination of the two." Gwen shrugged. "But that girl was here already, and Veronica came here because of her."

"Fine." Matthew waved off her words. "I don't give a damn about that. The point is—"

"I'm *not done*," Gwen hissed. "I'm so tired of you not listening to me. Just because I'm a woman and the youngest in the family doesn't mean I don't have thoughts and ideas of my own. Important ones."

Wow. So much was going on here, including a lot of built-up resentment. Hell, probably centuries' worth since Alex was over three hundred years old. I grimaced. I hated that little fact. Maybe I had daddy issues, but he didn't look old, so did that still count?

"Oh, don't worry." Alex chuckled dryly. "It has nothing to do with your gender or age."

"What is this?" Matthew glanced back and forth between his siblings. "After everything I've done for you both, this is what I get?"

"Stop." Gwen wrinkled her nose in disgust. "You're pissed because Alex put aside century-old biases to work with wolf shifters and an angel to save not only his soulmate but me and an innocent human. I was on the brink of losing my humanity and being demonized. That group is the reason I'm still myself and Veronica is alive."

"So you're in favor of working with the wolves?" Matthew's face scrunched up. "And angels? Those two races are our biggest threat to retaining control of Shadow Terrace, and you just...want to let them overtake us?"

Fear was the reason the vampires didn't want the shifters and angels here. It was insane to think about.

"The wolves have no problem with us going to Shadow Ridge." Gwen cleared her throat. "Maybe there's something to it."

Matthew's fangs shot out like lightning bolts. "Are you saying—"

"She's not saying anything." Alex crossed his arms. "She's making an observation."

"Yeah, sure." Gwen rolled her eyes. "Let's go with that."

This was an old discussion they'd been having for who knew how long, and here I was, brand new and trying to catch up. My brain was running on information overload, but they'd been overthinking whether to allow other supernaturals over here for too long. "I get you don't like me."

What are you doing? Alex tensed with concern. *I don't want him taking his anger out on you.*

It's a good thing you're here to protect me. If I wanted Alex and Matthew to accept me into their family, I needed to make my voice heard as Gwen had.

"See, that's what humans are like." Matthew shook his head. "They don't understand how things work."

"Maybe that's a good thing." They were so old they couldn't see the bigger picture. "Think about it. What other supernatural creature has lived as long as you?"

"Angels." Matthew laughed cockily. "If you were one of us, you would know."

"That's my point." I moved to stand beside Alex. "I may not know much about this world yet, but I will. And I know that humans—who live nowhere near as long as you—get set in their ways and stop thinking with an open mind. The wolves you knew from three or four hundred years ago aren't the same ones here today. How can you know their intentions if you won't listen to what they have to say?"

Gwen tilted her head, considering my words.

"Maybe that's how humans work," Matthew said condescendingly, "but we're supernatural. Things aren't the same here as they are for humans, so forgive me if I don't want to hear about your *ways*. The way things get done here is by having people owe us favors, which two wolf council members and an angel councilwoman's daughter now do."

Gwen laughed without humor. "It would've been better if I'd turned evil or died than for you to owe someone? I'm glad to know what my life is worth to you." She stalked off toward the exit.

"Gwen," Matthew groaned. "That's not what I meant."

"Oh, you did." She stopped and pivoted to face him. "You didn't say those words, but you don't want to owe them."

She had a point, but I knew Alex cared about her. Even when he'd told me to do what I had to survive, I'd felt the pain those words had caused. I imagined Matthew felt the same way. The difference between Matthew and his siblings was that Alex had a connection with me, and Gwen had come close to dying. Matthew hadn't been here to see it. I had a feeling things would've been different if he'd gotten here before all the shit had gone down. Or...I hoped so.

"This is an emotionally-charged situation." Those were the words my various wardens would use when a fight broke out in the group homes. "So feelings are heightened, and things are being said that normally wouldn't be said."

Alex stood closer to me and nodded. "She's right. Maybe we should let things settle. We have a lot to clean up." He gestured at the two bodies.

"Oh, and there's another one in the tunnel." I wasn't sure if he knew about that one.

"Another body?" Matthew asked, perplexed.

"Yeah, Darick." I shivered, remembering how I'd stabbed him in the chest. With Zaro, the shadow had controlled me. I couldn't use that excuse with Darick. "I killed him after he locked the gate to keep Rosemary and the others from getting to me."

I'm so sorry. Alex's guilt drifted through me. *You should've never been put in that situation.*

Every passing minute, Alex's guilt over completing our connection became clearer and clearer. My fear was that he would regret it; then, where would that leave me? I couldn't live without him. Not now.

Okay, I *could*. I was stronger than that. I'd been through hell and back, but the point was—I didn't want to. I wanted him, but if he didn't want to be with me, I'd figure it out. Strangely, the thought of never seeing or talking to Sterlyn and the others again hurt nearly as bad.

"Tonight has been rough on everyone." Alex wrapped an arm around me, pulling me to his side. "It's best if Gwen goes home and gets some rest. I'll take Veronica back to Sterlyn's so she can do the same. I'll message Joshua to come help you."

That worked. I wanted to check on Annie anyway.

Matthew clenched his jaw. "I do not think that's wise."

My heart dropped. Matthew would say that I needed to leave town, and Alex would agree. Tears threatened my eyes, but I blinked them away. I needed to hear the words.

"Since you've chosen to be with Veronica, she should come home with us." Matthew scrutinized me, his eyes cold.

"No." Alex shook his head. "Absolutely not. She's safer outside the city."

"Brother, your place is by my side in Shadow City." Matthew locked gazes with Alex in challenge. "Besides, you claimed her in the bar that night. That's how Eilam knew about her. Do you really think the news hasn't traveled? Any vampire who wants leverage over us knows about her. Even if you sent her away, she could be threatened or killed just because you noticed her. Because of your natural possessiveness, your enemies know you will care if they touch something you've claimed. And we all know you more than care about her since she's wearing your mark, and they will figure that out when they find her."

In other words, if Alex wanted me to stay alive, he was stuck with me. That rationale sat hard in my stomach.

"But taking her to the city—" Alex hung his head.

"You already made that decision." Matthew karate-chopped the air. "It's time for you to come home. You have council responsibilities, anyway."

"Fine." Alex sighed. "We'll come to Shadow City, but we have to run by Sterlyn and Griffin's to get her things."

"Then go." Matthew walked past Gwen, heading out of the room. "I'll meet you at home."

His footsteps drew farther away, and Gwen smiled sadly at Alex and me. "It'll be okay. I hate to admit it, but he's right. She's part of the royal family and hiding her will make us appear weak."

"But exposing her to Shadow City will make her more of a target," Alex said brokenly, and his regret slammed into me like an earthquake.

"Doesn't matter." Gwen yawned. "You already made that decision, and you know it."

My heart fractured more.

She'd turned halfway before stopping to focus on me. "I'm sorry about trying to...uh...kill you. It wasn't personal. I hope you can forgive me."

I wasn't sure how to respond, but I had to say something. "No, I get it. Eilam did everything he could to push you to that state. He seemed surprised that you didn't succumb right away, so thanks for trying not to hurt me."

"It wasn't all for you, but yeah, no problem." She smiled, looking breathtakingly gorgeous. "Let's never do this again."

I chuckled. "Deal."

"See you two soon." She turned and headed out the door, leaving Alex and me behind.

"Come on, let's go." He took my hand and led me toward the tunnels.

"Wait." I tugged on my hand, stopping him. "My car isn't there anymore. How are we supposed to get to Sterlyn's?"

"My car *is* there," he explained, pulling me toward

the tunnel once more. "When we realized you weren't there, the wolves and I ran here."

We walked through the tunnel in silence. The moldy concrete walls would forever be burned into my memory, and when the gate came into view, I kept my gaze upward, not wanting to see Darick's body. As we grew closer, I closed my eyes so I wouldn't see what I'd done.

Some things you couldn't come back from.

Alex guided me around Darick, aware of my feelings; they radiated through our shared connection. When the cool metal of the gate brushed my arm, I opened my eyes, knowing I was in the clear.

When we reached the ladder, I glanced up. When Darick had leaped with me in his arms, we'd fallen a good twenty feet. Wanting to escape the memories, I started to climb at a steady pace.

"Are you okay?" Alex asked softly, climbing close behind me.

Again, I didn't want to let him know how much I'd been affected. "I will be." That was the safest bet.

He didn't push the issue, and a minute later, I climbed through the opening and stepped out into the woods where the trees and darkness of the night hid us. The moon shone down, and the warm summer air caressed me, but even though we'd left the chilly tunnel, I felt cold. I took a deep breath. The scents of pine and sandalwood were comfortingly familiar, and I exhaled as I soaked in the normal, calming sounds of nocturnal animals scurrying through the brush.

When Alex reached the top, I couldn't hold off the

conversation any longer. I needed to know if he regretted completing the bond with me. Hell, I knew he did—I'd felt it through our connection. The mixture of guilt, regret, and something I couldn't distinguish told the complete story.

But I needed to hear him say it. I met his gaze and exhaled. "We need to talk."

CHAPTER FOUR

He closed his eyes. "I had a feeling you were going to say that." He ran his hands through his hair and moved away from the hole toward me.

Yeah, he looked about as excited as I was to have this conversation, but the sooner we got it over with, the quicker I could mend my breaking heart. "I could feel you back there," I said softly.

"I'm so sorry." He dropped his hands and pinched the bridge of his nose. "For all of this. I should have known better."

Those words stabbed me in the heart. My lungs quit working, and my throat became parched. I couldn't swallow. Even though I'd expected him to say something along those lines, I hadn't been prepared for it. "Is that how you really feel?" I wanted him to say no, but the pure agony etched into his face and the way his body sagged spoke louder than words.

"Vampires are selfish, and that's exactly what I was."

He rubbed his temples. "We are at constant war with our humanity as if our vampire nature is luring us to turn evil."

I stumbled back. I'd never want him to turn into the creature he was resisting becoming. "I didn't realize I was part of that equation." If my leaving would keep him more human, I had to do it. He couldn't give in to his demons over me.

"Of course, you are." He hurried to me and cupped my face with his palm, and his soft blue irises darkened with emotion. "But it's not fair of me to ask you to stay."

"What?" His words didn't make any sense.

"You deserve happiness and the kind of life I can't give you." He smiled sadly. "And I understand why you want that. I don't blame you for it."

He couldn't turn this around and blame me. I wouldn't let him. "That's not what I'm saying, and you know it. I don't regret anything. You're the one who feels guilty about completing our bond."

"I do." He dropped his hands to his sides. "If it weren't for me, you wouldn't have come so close to death. If something had happened to you—" He glanced away, unable to continue.

"But it didn't." He couldn't do that to himself. "Like Gwen said, either way, I would've been here because of Annie. You aren't responsible for that." None of this was his fault. "If you hadn't been there, Klyn would've fed from me and potentially killed me that first night. Annie and I are alive because of you."

"Maybe." He shrugged. "But I understand why you don't want to stay. This is a lot to take in."

My mind whirled. "Uh...I do want to stay, but you're the one who needs me to go."

He gasped. "Is that what you think?"

Hope sprang inside me, causing my heart to beat again. "Yes. I felt your regret, and if what you said about being selfish is true, I need to go. I don't want you to turn into the monster you've been fighting for over three hundred years."

His usual flirty smile spread across his face. "You *don't* want to go?"

Butterflies took flight in my stomach. "No. But I will for you."

"Then you're staying." He wrapped his arms around me, pulling me flush against his chest. "If you want to be here, there is no way in hell that I'm letting you go."

"But you said—"

He booped me on the nose. "Letting you go would be the most selfless thing I've ever done, and it would shatter my heart. To numb my pain, I would be tempted to embrace my inhuman side."

"How do you know that?" That sounded horrible, and I could never put him in that position. He was the most important person in my life, and I wanted what was best for him.

"Because it was hard enough when my parents died fifty years ago." Alex's head drooped. "Going rogue tempted Gwen, Matthew, and me. Fortunately, we had each other to rely on and got through the hard times of our lives together with our humanity intact. But losing you...I'd have no one to share that kind of pain with. No one here could understand it."

"Why did you feel so guilty and regretful?" I'd been so certain that he didn't want anything to do with me anymore.

"Your entire life has changed because of me," he said, his arms tightening around me. "Not only are you not going home with your sister, the best friend you came here and risked your life for, but you're giving up whatever future you had planned. I love you so damn much that it hurts to think you are doing that."

I laughed as my heart overflowed with happiness. We both had been so damn insecure that neither one of us had seen the real picture.

"Are you okay?" His forehead lined with concern as he watched me. "Did you break down there?" The corner of his mouth tipped upward.

"You do realize that Annie was planning to go away to college in about a month, right? Maybe she won't go away in August like she planned, but she will eventually." She wouldn't even be living at our house soon. "And Eliza has been pushing me to think about my future."

"Okay?" He pursed his lips. "And that makes you happy?"

"What? No." I placed my hand on his chest and glimpsed into his eyes. "Eliza works two jobs to support Annie and me, and we're still barely getting by even with all the hours I work as well. So, with Eliza always working, and with Annie gone—" I stopped.

He nibbled on his bottom lip. "I'm not following."

Apparently, I needed to clarify. "I never had future plans because I didn't know what I wanted to do. When I thought about my future, it was blank, full of doubt and indecision." I wasn't good at talking about my emotions. Maybe some of that was due to my childhood and being on my own for so long. But he'd bared his heart to me, and I needed to give that trust in return. "But ever since you, that's changed."

His eyes lit up, and he grinned. "Really? How so?"

"This place..." I pursed my lips. "Okay, maybe not *this* place—" I waved my hand in a circle, indicating the woods where I'd been kidnapped. "—but you, Sterlyn, Rosemary, Sierra, and even Griffin and Killian, feel like my home now."

"You're lumping me in with wolves and an angel?" He beamed.

"Yeah, and admit it." I stood on my tiptoes and brushed my lips against his. "You kinda like them after hanging out with them for a week."

"That is something I can never admit." He winked. "If Matthew ever got wind, he very well might kill me."

That sobered me. I felt overwhelmed by everything going on here. "Your death is something I will never find funny, even if you're joking. How would you feel if I said something like that?"

"I'd hate it." He scowled and his fingers dug into my sides. "I'm sorry." He buried his face in my hair and took a deep breath.

My annoyance vanished with that loving touch. Here

I'd been thinking the worst, and instead, we were wrapped in each other's arms, the way we should always be. "I thought you were breaking up with me."

"God, no." He pulled back and stared into my eyes. "I thought you regretted bonding with me. You had no clue what you were getting into until afterward."

"That's not true or fair." I ran my fingertips along his jaw, enjoying the feel of his scruff. "My connection to you was so overwhelming that, at times, I felt like I couldn't breathe. Yes, when your voice popped into my head the first time, I didn't expect it, but my feelings for you have solidified and become stronger. There is nowhere in the world I'd rather be than by your side."

"But being here puts you in so much danger." He placed his forehead against mine as he whispered, "I love you so much—that's why I should've let you go."

"I wouldn't have left." I needed him to realize that I cared about him as much as he did about me. My heart overflowed with love, and his feelings matched mine, giving us a high that I never wanted to end. "We are meant to be together. Fate decided it. Who are we to say no?"

He kissed me, stealing my breath away, but I wasn't complaining.

We needed this moment—us affirming how we felt for each other.

I love you, I pushed toward him, hoping he could hear it inside his head.

I love you too, he responded, and my heart was so full it could have exploded.

My hands slipped under his shirt as warmth flooded my body and desperation clawed inside me. I needed him now.

His body quivered under my touch.

Encouraged by his reaction, I slipped my tongue inside his mouth.

We're in the woods, he said, trying to stay rational.

Yeah, fuck that. *So?* I kissed down his throat, feeling his heart thumping against my mouth.

All the books maintained vampires were dead, but Alex was proof they weren't. His heart beat the same as mine.

Veronica, he groaned.

I raked my teeth against his skin.

He hissed, and his muscles tightened beneath my hand. His hand slipped under my shirt and cupped my breast.

Are we alone? I asked. I bit him harder as an overwhelming urge began taking over, and something guided me to continue. Blood welled from the spot, and I licked it.

Yes. He moaned loudly and pressed himself against me. *We are, but you deserve something better than this.*

Maybe. I tasted his blood. It reminded me of syrup but so much better. The warmth and sweet flavor exploded on my tongue, and I didn't want to stop. *But I don't want a bed. I want you right now.*

Oh, dear God. He cradled my head, holding me there. *That feels so damn good.* His other hand caressed my nipple.

Need clenched inside me, and I pulled away. Dragging him to the ground, I straddled his legs.

He scooted backward to a grassy area against a tree trunk and paused. *Are you sure?*

I need you. I wasn't sure if it was the near-death experience I'd just gone through, our declarations of love for each other, the taste of his blood on my tongue, or all of it combined, but I was desperate. *You'll hear if someone or something is coming, right?*

He nodded as his hands gripped my legs.

Then I don't see a problem. I moved back to unfasten his belt and jeans. *Do you?*

Not at all. He growled while pink bled into his eyes. He lifted his hips and pulled down his jeans and boxers, and I paused to look at him.

He was so gorgeous, and every inch of him was mine.

And I did mean every inch.

Savoring the way his eyes continued to darken, I removed my jeans and panties then straddled him, ready for him.

He slipped inside me, filling me completely, and we moved together.

Grass and tree bark dug into my knees, the sting fueling my desire, and I quickened the pace. His hands raised my shirt, and he unfastened my bra, lifting it with my shirt.

Leaning over, he captured one nipple in his mouth and flicked his tongue over the peak. I increased our rhythm even more. This might not be like our first time, but it was more intense than ever, like our connection was desperate to seal everything we'd said.

The pressure built between us, and I threw my head back as sensations overwhelmed me.

"Alex," I moaned.

Damn, I like you saying my name. He grabbed my hips, pumping into me.

My body tipped over the edge, and I kissed him even harder. His tongue stroked mine, and his body convulsed underneath me, strengthening my orgasm.

We stilled to catch our breath, and our emotions collided through the bond. He peppered my face with kisses and played with the ends of my hair. "That was amazing."

Strangely, he made me feel sexy. I'd never felt that way before. "Yeah." I half smiled then remembered what I'd done first and grimaced. "And sorry about—" Unable to finish that sentence, I gestured at his neck.

"Drinking my blood?" he asked with a crooked grin.

"Yeah." My face burned hot.

"Don't be." He kissed me deeply again. *I loved it.*

Really? I didn't... I trailed off.

"It's probably because we're bonded and some of my vampiric desires are clouding your mind." He smiled reassuringly.

I bet he was used to doing that while having sex. I placed a hand on his chest, pushing him back. "Has me being human not made things as pleasurable—"

He placed a finger over my lips and rasped, "No one

has ever tasted my blood before. We save that for our mates. It's too meaningful to us."

"Really?" That was such a relief. At least, in one way, I was a first for him.

"Yes." He caught my waist and lifted me. "I hate to ruin this moment, but we are in the woods, and Matthew will worry if we aren't there soon. I'd hate for him to send someone searching for us."

Great, that comment put a damper on things. But I could think of one way to make it better. "When we get to Shadow City, I'm assuming we can do this again." I stood and put on my panties and jeans.

"Oh, that's a given." He kissed me and got dressed too. "Many times over."

"Now *that* sounds like a plan." I would never get enough of him, not in a million years.

Hand in hand, we headed to his car.

We pulled up at Sterlyn's around midnight, and between the two parked cars belonging to Annie and me, the driveway was full. Alex parked his Mercedes SUV at the curb, and I got out.

With Alex on my heels, I hurried to the door, wanting to check on Annie. I didn't regret our time in the woods and would've done it all over again, but now that we were close, I wanted Annie to leave and fast.

Without knocking, I swung open the front door into the living room. I scanned the room, already familiar with the pearl-gray couch on one side of the room and the flat-screen television mounted on the opposite wall. The four wolves and Rosemary stood in front of the matching loveseat, which sat perpendicular to the couch and across from the windows with white blinds. To the right of the windows was a glass door that led to the backyard. Annie stood in front of it, white as a ghost, staring at her reflection in the glass.

Sterlyn turned to Alex and me and said, "Thank God you're here."

CHAPTER FIVE

Dread coursed through me. I couldn't remember a time when Sterlyn had sounded so stressed. Granted, I hadn't known her very long, but we'd faced some horrible situations. "What's wrong?" I returned my attention to Annie, knowing it had to do with her.

"When we got back, Rosemary stayed here with Annie while the rest of us went into the bedrooms to shift back into human form." Sterlyn rubbed her arms as concern filled her lavender-silver eyes. "When we came back out, we found her like this." She pushed her long silver hair over her shoulder.

"Okay...?" Alex said. "What's the problem?"

However, I already knew. I'd seen her like this once before when that neighborhood dog had gotten run over. She'd loved the dog, and she'd been sneaking it food and water. When it died, she'd retreated within herself and ignored the outside world for days.

I'd brought her out of her fugue state by dragging her

to a pet store to see puppies. She'd broken down and told me about a part of her past I hadn't known. She'd always felt incomplete, like part of her was missing, but in third grade, she had a classmate—Suzy—who became her best friend. One day, when they were playing soccer, Annie kicked the ball into the road, and Suzy chased after it, not looking for traffic. She was hit by a car and died on the spot. Losing the dog had been like losing Suzy all over again.

"She's withdrawn." I approached Annie slowly. Her carefree and loving attitude was genuine, but it also helped cover up the broken girl inside. That was one reason I was determined to help her make a good life for herself. She deserved it for retaining her amazing heart after everything she'd gone through.

Sierra's gray eyes focused on the angel. "I asked Rosemary what she said to piss her off, but she swears she did nothing." Sierra lowered her voice and draped her dirty-blond hair over her shoulder like a barrier, pretending she didn't want Rosemary to hear what she said next, but she purposely spoke in a whisper loud enough that even my human ears heard her. "Even though Rosemary has gotten better with reading social cues, she has a long way to go."

"I didn't say a word to her," Rosemary growled, glaring at Sierra. "So, there is no possible way you can blame me for this."

"Don't be so insolent." Killian sighed and scratched his head, further disheveling his cappuccino hair. "You know Sierra has a knack for twisting everyone's words

and actions." His lips mashed into a line, making his chis-
eled face more handsome.

He and Sierra always bantered, but I wished they'd
be more serious; like Griffin. "Can you command those
two to stop bickering?"

"If I could, I would." Griffin rolled his eyes.

My brows pulled together, and I connected with
Alex, *Wait. Aren't they pack?*

They aren't. Alex pursed his lips. *Sterlyn didn't join
Griffin's pack when they mated, and Killian submitted to
Griffin and Sterlyn as individuals, which allows him to
link with both of them. They are still, technically, three
separate packs.*

Another little fact that I didn't know, but now wasn't
the time to dwell on it.

Griffin frowned as his hazel eyes glanced back and
forth between us and Annie, resulting in a piece of his
honey-gold hair falling in his face. The golden scruff on
his chin had grown longer, probably from being in his
animal form. Standing at six and a half feet, he was the
tallest person in the room. The muscles in his crossed
arms bulged. "Can you help her?"

I hoped so. All the dead bodies she'd seen must have
reminded her of Suzy's death. Alex had told her not to
remember anything about the supernatural world once
she'd left this area, but she was still here and hadn't
forgotten the deaths yet. I suspected she was re-experi-
encing the trauma. "Let me try."

Determined, I slowly approached her. I didn't want
to startle her and cause her to retreat. "Annie," I said

gently, approaching her like she might attack at any second.

Like the day the dog had died, she didn't react. Not a nod, a flinch, or any acknowledgment that I was there. Maybe I should've gone with Sterlyn and the others instead of staying at the blood bank with Alex. "You're safe now."

Her head shook, the motion so small I wouldn't have noticed if I hadn't been watching her so intently. Good, she was somewhat aware.

"We need to get you home."

That was the best place for her. I glanced at Alex. "I know you answered this, but I have to ask again. She'll forget about the dead bodies once she's gone, right?"

"She will forget them." He stayed in the foyer. "I told her what she would remember."

Then, instead of dragging out her pain, we needed to get her out of here. That would fix everything. "Seeing the bodies probably triggered a childhood memory of her friend's death." I hated that she had that memory stored away somewhere. She was good at blocking it out until something reminded her of Suzy. "Can you make her forget them entirely so she can drive home?" I hated to mess with her mind, but it was for her own good. She wouldn't remember it all anyway.

"Yeah, I can do that." Alex passed the others on his way to me. He was shorter than Griffin and Killian by several inches. Sometimes, I forgot about that until they were close together.

I touched Annie's shoulder, wanting her to know I

was there as Alex stopped by my side. He reached out to touch Annie's cheek, and just like last time, irrational jealousy coursed through me, and I growled. Part of me wanted to slap my sister, while the other part knew I was being ridiculous. He was helping her. Why did it bother me when he touched her? All he was going to do was stare into her eyes and work his magic.

"Easy, girl." Sierra snorted as she nabbed my arm and tugged me away from Annie and Alex.

"Thanks," I said, not fighting her. "Why does it bother me so much? He's not doing anything wrong."

"It's the new mate bond," Sterlyn reassured me and leaned her head on Griffin's shoulder. "We're all the same way with our mates. We don't want them touching anyone, or anyone else touching them, but it's significantly worse when newly mated."

"Add in the fact you're human." Rosemary peered over Sierra's head directly at me. That was how much taller she was than the shifter. "And you have a supernatural connection—you probably can't control yourself since it's a powerful bond that a human can't withstand."

Yup, there was Rosemary's blunt nature coming into play. I stewed over their words for a second. "Because I'm human, I react to the bond more strongly than if I were supernatural?"

"That's my guess. Think of it like a small human trying to walk." Rosemary shuddered. "They fall and get all banged up because they don't know any better."

"You mean babies?" Sierra deadpanned.

Rosemary nodded. "Yeah, that's what I said."

They aren't shutting up. The annoyance rolling off Alex would have been clear even without our link. His tone softened in our connection. *And I like it when you're possessive. It just reinforces our connection and that we're committed to each other in the most sacred of ways.*

I wasn't sure I agreed with that sentiment. I wanted a normal, healthy relationship built on trust, not insecurities. "Guys, seriously. Be quiet."

Sierra's face grew serious. "Yeah, sure."

At least, she understood. Maybe humor was her way of handling a situation until it got to a point like this. I understood that and felt my criticism of her soften.

"Annie." Alex touched her chin, forcing her eyes to connect with his. "I need you to forget about the bodies you saw earlier today."

She nodded, finally responding to someone. "I'd very much like that."

Wait. *Can you make her forget about her friend's death too?* Maybe we could heal the hurt and pain she'd grown up with and make her whole. If I were her, I'd want that gift.

I hate telling you no, especially when your request is filled with good intentions, but I can't do that. Alex's regret wafted to me.

That didn't make any sense. *Why? She could forget about a horrible part of her past.*

Exactly. Alex dropped his hand, releasing Annie from his hold. *The farther back I go to change her memories, the more unstable her mind will become. These last few weeks are recent enough that there won't be many side effects but going back to her childhood... That's different. Also, her friend's death molded her into who she is today, for better or worse. Erasing that would make her a different person, one you and Eliza wouldn't recognize.*

Once again, I didn't know or understand about the supernatural world. Everything he'd said made complete sense. *Eliza would still remember it, and Annie wouldn't.* Even if they didn't talk about it daily, the topic often came up, usually around Suzy's death date. Unless we were willing to mess with Eliza's mind too, we needed to keep that memory intact. Now I felt bad for even suggesting he erase it.

Alex walked over and pulled me into his arms. He kissed the top of my head. *You shouldn't feel guilty about any of this. You're learning how everything works here. You didn't know.*

Thank you for telling me no. He could've done it for me, fearing I'd get upset, but he'd stood by his convictions, and I fell a little more in love with him. It shouldn't have been possible, but there it was. *You're a good man.*

If I didn't know you'd be upset with the outcome, I would do it for you. He leaned back and brushed his lips against mine. *I will always have your best interests at heart. And can I add that I'm honored I get to teach you all about my world?*

I like it too. If I was going to have any teacher, I wanted it to be him. I kissed him, enjoying his taste.

"Oh my God, Ronnie." Annie gasped beside me. "What's gotten into you?"

She sounded normal, and laughter bubbled in my throat as I pulled back.

"Uh...do you really want her to answer that question?" Sierra asked, her snark reappearing at the first opportunity. "Because if you haven't figured it out from that kiss, then we'll need to have a birds-and-bees conversation." She waggled her eyebrows at my friend.

Sterlyn burst into laughter as Rosemary shook her head.

The dark angel wrinkled her nose, "And you say *I* say things I shouldn't."

"You can tell Sierra's siblings are male." Killian stretched, raising his hands over his head, and his dark-chocolate eyes lit with mirth. "She has the humor of a twelve-year-old boy, conveying her maturity level."

"Bite me." Sierra stuck out her tongue at him.

Now that Annie had snapped out of her fugue state, I enjoyed their back and forth.

"First off, do you think it's wise to say that with a vampire in the room?" Rosemary asked in all seriousness. "And two, what is it with all the sex humor? So what if they have sex?"

"She's just jealous." Sterlyn chuckled. "She's the only one not getting any."

Oh, dear God, there was no way Sierra would let that slide.

Instead of a smart retort, Sierra's mouth dropped. "Rosemary is single too."

Rosemary smirked. "That doesn't mean I'm not having sex."

"No wonder you like them." Annie laughed and snagged my arm, unraveling me from Alex. "But you—" She narrowed her eyes at him and waved a hand as suspicion took hold. "I don't care if you are a vampire, if you hurt my sister, I will kill you. Or re-kill you. Whatever."

"And there, Annie just stole my heart." Sierra laid her hand on her chest. "A protective sibling who wants to eliminate a vampire. There's nothing better than that."

"Maybe you're into girls," Griffin suggested. "That might be why you can't find anyone to sleep with."

"Hey, there are plenty of attractive girls, believe me." Sierra gestured at Sterlyn, Rosemary, me, and Annie. "Unfortunately, I'm straight."

"Unfortunately." Killian pursed his lips. "So, you've thought about it?"

"As fun as this conversation is"—this could become a long-winded distraction if I didn't demand their focus —"Annie needs to go back home to Eliza. She's worried, and Alex and I need to get to Shadow City."

"Wait." Rosemary rubbed her bottom lip. "You're taking Ronnie to Shadow City? She's a human."

"I know, but since we completed the bond, the best way to protect her is to keep her by my side." Alex turned to me. "Matthew is also demanding it. Unless I'm willing to widen the rift between us, this is what we have to do."

"But—" Griffin started, and I cut him off, the decision already made.

"Look, I get your concern, but Matthew is right. I'm Alex's soulmate, and I'm not going anywhere. My place is beside him in all ways."

Even if I wasn't a vampire, I was an equal, and one way or another, I'd make everyone see that.

"No, it's a smart move." Sterlyn paced in front of us. "Risky, but the strongest move you could make. By taking her to Shadow City and integrating her into society, you'll control the narrative with your people and the council."

"True." Rosemary considered Sterlyn's words. "And you'll have a majority vote since you'll have the wolf shifters' votes, the vampires' votes, and, once I speak with my mom, two angel votes."

"Hold on." I was missing a piece of information. "Why would the council have a say?"

"Because they must agree to let someone into the city," Griffin answered. "As soon as you walk through that barrier, an emergency hearing will be called. Anyone who doesn't vote in your favor will be highly pissed about your presence. They don't want other supernaturals moving in, and for a human to..." He trailed off, not needing to finish that thought.

Great. And here I'd thought we'd just go to Alex's house and have the rest of the night to recuperate. This new scenario made me more eager to get going. "Then we better move." I hugged Annie, breathing in her faint jasmine scent.

"Sounds like you have a lot to do." Her arms tightened around me harder. "Thank you so much for protecting me." Her voice cracked with emotion.

"I love you," I whispered with tears flooding my eyes. "I'll do everything I can to make sure you stay safe."

"Since you two obviously need to be in Shadow City tonight, Annie can stay with me," Killian offered.

"No, I want to go home." Annie hugged herself. "I... I've got to get away from here if Ronnie isn't staying."

"Okay," Killian said and headed to the front door. "I'll get my keys and follow you home."

His words filled me with relief. I hadn't realized I was worried about her making it back to Eliza's unharmed. "Are you sure?"

"Yeah." He smiled at me. "I'll follow her there and come right back." He turned to Annie. "Why don't you get in your car, and I'll be out in a moment?"

"Okay." Annie sounded eager, ready to go home. "And thank you."

"Go say goodbye, and I'll get your things." Alex kissed my forehead and nodded at Annie. "It was nice meeting you."

Are you sure? I didn't feel right making Alex pack the few clothes I had.

He nodded. *Yup. She wants to talk to you anyway.* He disappeared down the hall.

Annie said goodbye to Sterlyn and the others and looped her arm through mine, dragging me to the door. She whispered, "Let's go outside. Now."

CHAPTER SIX

A nnie and I walked to her vehicle. On the right side of the house, blinds shifted in the room Alex and I had been staying in. Soft blue eyes stared out from between the spaces.

I thought you were getting our stuff together? A thrill ran through me at him watching us. If it had been any other guy, I would've been put off by his clinginess, but with Alex, I didn't want it any other way. All the stress was helping our bond become more stable since my volatile emotions strengthened it.

He didn't even try to pretend he wasn't spying. His eyes took on a slight glow. *You were just captured and nearly killed...again. Excuse me if I want to keep an eye on you while you're outside with no one around. Besides, you aren't upset. I'd know if you were.*

"Earth to Ronnie." Annie snapped her fingers in front of my face. "Is something wrong?" She glanced at the window, and her brows drew together.

She couldn't see him, but how? His eyes were clear as day. Unless I was channeling Alex's supernatural urges and abilities again...

"No, sorry." I forced my attention back to her. "It's been a crazy day."

"Day?" Annie rubbed her hands on her neck where Eilam had bitten her and leaned against her black Honda Civic. "How about a crazy month? God, I was so damn stupid."

"In all fairness, you didn't know what was happening." This was something she didn't need to beat herself up about. "You came here to check out a college you were interested in, and a vampire messed with your mind."

"Still, because of me, you're in this situation." She gestured to the house and shook her head. "And I think they've done the same thing to you."

"What do you mean?"

Annie exhaled. "Don't get mad, but I think you should come home with me. I think Alex is messing with your mind like Eilam messed with mine."

"No, Alex would never do something like that to me."

She raised her hand. "I said the same thing about Eilam not even an hour ago. So, sorry if I find that hard to believe."

"Alex isn't like Eilam." I tried to keep my voice level, but anger leaked through. "He saved us. Eilam only wanted to feed from you and use you as a sex toy." I grimaced, immediately regretting the words I couldn't take back.

Hands fisted, Annie paused as if trying to remain

calm. "Thanks for your bluntness, but you've got one part wrong. He didn't have sex with me. Thank God. He said humans weren't worthy."

Relief overwhelmed me, and tears blurred my eyes. He'd still violated her, but at least, sexual assault was off the table. What she'd been through was bad enough. "I'm sorry. It's just...Alex isn't anything like him, and it upsets me that you would compare the two."

"But that's my point. You've never wanted to be serious with a guy before. Why him? Right after what I just went through..." She blew a raspberry. "I don't want you to make the same mistake I did. Just...come back home and see if you still feel the same way. Maybe distance will give you a different perspective."

Treading carefully, I organized my thoughts. "First off, if that was true, distance wouldn't help. Remember, you kept coming back to Eilam. And two, I know he didn't manipulate my mind."

"Oh, really?" She huffed. "How?"

"Because he tried, and it didn't work." The day after he'd kissed me at Thirsty's flashed in my memory. On our way out of Shadow Terrace, he'd stopped the car, and we'd gotten into a huge argument. He'd tried to erase my memory of him so I would go home to safety, but my mind had stayed firmly intact, shocking him.

"Come on, Ronnie." She rolled her eyes. "If vampires can mess with our minds, that might not have even happened."

But I knew he hadn't. "He wasn't lying. Sterlyn—"

"You're banking everything on people you just met."

Annie's eyes flashed with anger, and she gritted her teeth. "If you're going to trust anyone, it should be me. I've had your back for the past six years. They haven't."

My mind reeled. I didn't want to hurt her, but she didn't understand. "I love you so much. No one could ever take your place—"

"Then come home." She pushed off the car and turned to climb into the driver's seat.

I touched her shoulder, holding her in place. "I wasn't finished."

"Yeah." Her chuckle held an edge as she turned back around and tapped her fingers on her legs. "Please, continue."

She'd never acted like this with me before. It hurt, but I knew where I belonged. "This place fills a missing piece inside me. I know it sounds crazy, but this is where I'm meant to be, even if Alex weren't involved."

Annie's jaw twitched. "But—"

"Alex is my forever." I wished it was easier to make it clear to her. I wished she could believe this was the real Ronnie speaking, but after what she'd gone through, I couldn't blame her for doubting me. If I were in her shoes, I'd feel the same way. "He's my soulmate, and the others...they're my friends."

"This place isn't meant for us, Ronnie." Annie pointed at her bite mark. "We aren't supernatural. We weren't made for this world."

"I am." As I said the words, I realized how much I meant them. This was my home. I wouldn't feel right in my own skin staying with Eliza. "I get that it's crazy because I'm human, but this is where I'm supposed to be." I motioned to my neck. "I don't have the same marks as you. He isn't feeding from me."

"You know what?" Anger replaced her hurt. "Fine. Stay. Since these people are so much more important than your own family."

"That's not fair." I forced myself to hold back my anger. She didn't understand. "You and Eliza mean the world to me, but I have to do this for myself." For the first time in my life, I was putting myself first. Annie was used to me bending over backward for her.

The front door opened, and Killian exited the house. He dangled his keys from his hand and motioned to the hunter-green house next door. "My car is in my garage. Are you ready?"

"More than ready." Turning her back to me, Annie swung open the car door and got in.

Killian's eyebrows lifted, and he gave me a questioning glance.

I didn't want to explain it to him, especially in front of Annie.

He saluted and said to Annie, "Go ahead and pull out. I'll be behind you in a flash."

"Got it." She slammed the door shut and started the car.

As she pulled out of the driveway, she didn't even glance my way.

I watched her go, part of me hurting. I hated that we had parted on this bitter note. She cared and wanted to protect me, but I didn't need that. Leaving with her wasn't an option. The pain would have been unbearable.

I called after Killian, "Let someone know when you and Annie make it there safely. Please."

He gave me a thumbs-up and disappeared into his house. His garage door soon rumbled open.

The front door opened again, and the *yank* in my chest informed me who it was. Within seconds, Alex appeared beside me, carrying a bag over his shoulder. He didn't say a word as I watched my sister and best friend drive away with Killian behind her.

"You knew what she wanted to talk about, didn't you?" I kept my attention on the cars until they disappeared around a corner.

He nodded. "I had a pretty good guess."

Yet, he hadn't warned me. "Why did you let me come out here, then? Why didn't you join me?"

"Because you care about her, and she loves you," he explained and took my hand. "You two needed to have that conversation without me."

"But she accused you of—"

Softly smiling, he ran his fingers through my hair. "She has a right to be concerned. It could've happened, and it would be an insult to her intelligence to think she wouldn't consider that after everything she's been through. She probably felt as strongly about Eilam as you do about me."

"Our connection is real." I didn't like the comparison.

"It is." He lowered his forehead to mine. "And theirs

wasn't. That doesn't mean she didn't think it was real in the moment."

He was right. I hated to even consider that she thought my feelings for Alex were manipulated like hers had been for Eilam. I closed my eyes as the hurt intensified. "She's mad at me."

"No, she's not," he said and kissed my nose. "She's hurt. She's afraid she's lost you to us. That we might make you forget her like she forgot you. Fear is making her act that way."

"That doesn't make it better." I loved her so much, but she wasn't the center of my world anymore. My time here had changed that, and when I thought about the future, it involved me and Alex—together. Before, it had been all about Annie.

I lifted my head to stare into his gorgeous eyes. He took my breath away, and it was more than just his perfect face and body. He cared about me and put my needs before his own. Even before we'd accepted our connection, he'd risked his neck to save me from Klyn, then from the mystery aggressor outside my hotel room on my first night in town to find Annie. "Who tried to attack me that night in the hotel?" I'd never gotten closure to that question, and I didn't know why I hadn't asked before now.

He pursed his lips. "That's random."

"Not really." I kissed him. "I was thinking about how you'd protected me before we ever spoke, and it made me think of that night."

"I didn't understand my instincts then." He smiled.

"But I couldn't stop myself. The thought of something happening to you made it feel like the world would never be the same."

He was a hopeless romantic, and I hoped he would never change. "Not answering my question."

"Fine." His hand slid down to my neck, his palm resting over my heartbeat. "It was the bellhop."

Maybe it was the way the bellhop and the desk clerk had acted when I'd entered the hotel lobby, but I wasn't surprised. The way he'd watched me had made my skin crawl, and the clerk had asked me if I was alone. It made complete sense now. "Of course. Still, anyone staying in the hotel would have heard him attack. Why did no one else help?"

"Humans are brought to the blood bank at night to make their donations. The process is similar to other blood banks, except the vampires make them forget once it's done. Most of the guests were gone, and the bellhop took advantage of that fact. No one was near enough to hear him when he tried to break down your door. He was part of Eilam's crew." Pink bled into his irises.

No wonder he'd wanted me to leave town that night. "How did you know to check on me?"

"I'd heard rumblings while I was at Thirsty's about a hotel employee drinking from humans, and when I drove by and saw your car parked in their lot, I had to check on you." Alex licked his lips. "Just before you came in, I was meeting with Blade—he's what you'd consider the mayor of Shadow Terrace—and the bar's owner, Cedric, to figure out who was involved in blood trafficking. There were rumors that some of the vampires who picked up humans at the bar were part of it. You came in looking for Annie, and it helped us figure things out a lot faster."

"Did the bellhop lead you to Eilam?" Something still wasn't clicking, but the fact that he was confiding in me reaffirmed that he knew we were an official team.

"No." He grimaced. "I killed him before I could ask him anything. I started digging around into Annie's visit to Shadow Ridge University, and Eilam's name came to light."

A shiver ran down my spine. "He was openly drinking from her in the bar, even in front of you." If Eilam had been hiding, why the hell had he done that?

Alex glanced skyward. "He knew he'd been caught and was flaunting it. I was going to take him to jail right then and there, but then you waltzed in."

"You wanted to kill me." I laughed. He'd been so damn angry that day.

He shoved he bag out of the way and pulled me against him. "No. I wanted to spank you. You love walking into danger."

"I don't regret a second of it." That day, everything had changed between us. "I got the best damn kiss of my entire life because of it."

He groaned, capturing my lips with his. "Then I've got a lot of practicing to do to top it."

"Hmm." I kissed him back and wrestled the grin that wanted to spread across my face. "That sounds like a whole lot of work. Not sure if I'm up for the challenge."

He licked my lips and thought to me, *I guess I'd better be convincing.*

The front door opened, and Sierra coughed. "Dear God. Please stop. I can smell the arousal all the way over here, and you're outside."

"Then go back inside," Alex hissed.

Her footsteps came closer. "Oh, hell no. You said you guys were heading back to Shadow City, so it should've been safe for me to hang out here without having to endure your foreplay." She cleared her throat, empha-sizing that she wasn't leaving. "Besides, I can't go back in. Griffin kicked me out, saying I was preventing them from leaving."

The garage door opened, proving her point.

Begrudgingly, I pulled away from Alex. We needed to get to Shadow City before Matthew freaked. It was already past one in the morning.

Alex glowered at Sierra, and I noticed they were acting like friends and not just temporary allies.

"Dude, I thought we were in a hurry," Griffin said as he walked to the driver's door.

"We are." Alex placed a hand on the small of my back and led me to his car.

I paused. "What should we do with my car?" I didn't want it to be in Griffin and Sterlyn's way, but I had a feeling we needed to take Alex's car into the city.

"It's fine there." Sterlyn opened her door. "We can get out without issue."

"You better keep her safe." Sierra stared Alex down. "And bring her back soon."

Alex adjusted the strap of the bag on his arm. "I will protect her with my life, and don't worry. I want to come back here as fast as we can."

I got into the Mercedes. Throwing my bag in the back, he climbed into the driver's seat. I waved at Sierra as we pulled away from the house.

The neighborhood disappeared in the rearview mirror, and my heart pounded.

In silence, Alex drove us into the heart of town, toward the university. Shadow Ridge brimmed with nightlife, and people thronged the streets. Large groups headed into the various restaurants and bars as we passed, seemingly without a care in the world. Many appeared to be around my age, although that wasn't necessarily true—most supernaturals appeared young. I couldn't really tell humans from supernaturals yet.

Nice to know that on this side of the river, the social scene wasn't so different from the one at home.

I settled into the seat, not sure how long it would take us to reach Shadow City.

Alex slowed, allowing Griffin to move in front of us. "This way, we won't have to get out of the car," he explained. "Griffin and Sterlyn can connect with the pack behind the city wall and get us through."

Suddenly, Griffin made a sharp right, and the Navigator raced toward the river.

"What the hell?" I shouted, my body tensing. "They turned off the road." I closed my eyes, not wanting to see the impact.

CHAPTER SEVEN

"It's the way to Shadow City," Alex said with confusion and turned our car to follow them.

My eyes opened, and I reached across the center console. "That can't be right. The car's too heavy. We'll sink." This had to be a nightmare. I'd narrowly escaped death only to die in a sinking car. Oh, hell no.

I unlocked my door, ready to jump out, as blood rushed through my ears.

"No, it's fine." Alex wrapped an arm around my shoulders as he continued toward the embankment. "I forgot that you can't see the bridge. Once our vehicles reach the magical barrier, we'll disappear from human sight as well."

As I braced myself for impact, the car continued to drive smoothly, and a colossal, sturdy cement bridge magically appeared in front of us with a domelike structure looming in the distance. "What the—" I glanced at the top of the bridge. It reminded me of pictures I'd seen of the Golden Gate Bridge in California. "How could I not see this?" I forced myself to exhale now that we weren't in any danger.

"It's spelled by the witch coven in the city." Alex rubbed my shoulder. "Only supernaturals can see it. Humans only see the Tennessee River flowing by, but now that you've broken through the protection barrier, you can see the city as I do."

The area where the bridge and city dome sat had looked like water to me only moments ago, and the river was eight times wider than I'd thought. In the center of the river stood hulking walls that were over one hundred stories high with an emblem embossed on them over and over. The emblem was simple yet breathtaking. The picture was of a skyline, and over the tallest two skyscrapers, an oversized paw print floated in the air. "Why is there a wolf print on top? Why is only one race identified in the emblem?" This was a supernatural city, so it seemed strange that only one race would be represented.

"Because of the silver wolves." Alex chuckled. "To make a long story short, Sterlyn is an angelic wolf. Rosemary's mother, Yelahiah, is the sister of the angel who reproduced with a wolf. He was murdered for that centuries ago, and Yelahiah demanded that her family be represented somehow. There was a lot of animosity among the angels, and she wanted the wolf paw print to remind her of the family she'd lost."

"There's so much history." I sat back in my seat and leaned forward, examining the top of the expansive glass dome. "I'm assuming that's to prevent anyone who can fly from getting in?"

"Yep, that's right. Many supernaturals can fly." He placed his hand on my thigh. "Angels, as you know, fly, and there are bird shifters and several others I've never seen but have heard stories about, mostly because they live in the Fae Realm, such as dragons, harpies, gargoyles, and many more."

"Whoa, there's another realm?" The world was so much bigger than I'd ever realized. It was both amazing and terrifying. "Do any Fae Realm people live on Earth?" So many myths existed that I assumed people had seen them throughout history.

"Apparently, there are some dragons now tied to Earth. They're shifters in this realm, like wolves, so they appear human." Alex shrugged. "I've never met one, but a bear shifter who worked for one of the former council members somehow left the city—despite it being in lockdown—to help the fae dragon king find the dragons who live here. That was before the handful of us were allowed to leave, but the bear was captured by the dragon shifters he was hunting and a group of their allies. A Shadow Ridge wolf went to pick him up to bring him back to Shadow City. The bear shifter went on and on about centaurs, dragons, vampires, and wolves, but before the Shadow Ridge wolf and the bear got back to the city, they got into a wreck, and the bear disappeared again. He ran off and hasn't been caught again."

The more I learned about this world, the crazier it

sounded. And I'd thought humans were dramatic; this went way beyond that. "What's the strongest race?"

"The angels, but not when the rest of us work together." Alex slowed down about a hundred yards from the city's main entrance where a section of the bridge was raised to prevent anyone from getting inside. "Shadow City was intended as a refuge for supernaturals, but the angels intervened, allowing only the strongest to live within the city. They wanted to rule over the most supreme members of all the races. Their attempt to control everyone caused a revolt. We learned that when the races banded together to fight the angels, we could defeat them."

That reinforced what I'd grown up hearing my entire life: if everyone worked together for the greater good, nothing could stand in their way. It had always sounded cheesy. Hell, it still did, but I, Alex, the wolf shifters, and Rosemary were already working together. If that didn't prove the theory, not much would. "It'll take a minute to wrap my head around all this."

"I know." Alex stopped the car behind Griffin's and rolled down his window, waving a hand. "But the more you know, the less the council can use you against me. They'll try to prove that you aren't meant to be part of this world."

Yeah, I'd had a feeling that would happen. Our being together had been a fight from the beginning. "We'll prove them wrong." We had to, or I'd die trying.

"Of course, we will." Alex pushed a piece of my hair

behind my ear. "And if they don't accept it, we'll leave and make a life for ourselves somewhere else."

Based on what Matthew had said, I doubted that could happen. He'd made it sound like people would hunt me down, and God knew what else, if Alex and I left. There were some things you couldn't hide from, but I didn't want to burst Alex's bubble. "What if the guards don't let me inside?"

"They will." Alex took my hand. "Between Griffin, Sterlyn, and me, they won't risk pissing off three council members in one sitting."

Gears ground, and the draw bridge lowered. The cement door began to lift. The process was slow and loud, even to me, as if the weight of the door was practically too much. I kept my hands in my lap, not wanting to come off like I already couldn't handle being here.

Inch by inch, the city came into view, and I'd never seen anything like it, not even in pictures. It was about the same size as downtown Lexington, and the buildings were clean and sleek and spread across the skyline. They soared upward in straight, precise lines, and a few looked like they were made of golden glass. A medium-sized building with a huge, round, purple-stained roof caught my eye. This was the skyline in the city emblem. Only the wolf print hovering in the sky was missing, which I wouldn't have been surprised to see.

"Wow." I wasn't sure what else to say. "This can't be real. I've never seen glass reflect like that." Even with the moon high in the sky, the streets were full of people. They all wore modern clothing, too. I didn't know why, but I'd expected them to wear clothes from a thousand years ago. Clearly, they'd kept up with the times.

There weren't any streetlights like at home. The only lights came from the sky and the buildings, but the people didn't struggle to see. Most surprising, there weren't any vehicles on the road, besides Griffin's and Alex's. "Don't people have cars here?"

"Only those who leave the city regularly." Alex grinned, watching me for a second. "We have a section of woods where the shifters can run and roam with wildlife. Anything we can't get from the city is funneled in through one of the gates."

"So that's why you have modern things?" I couldn't get over how the walled-off city seemed more cutting edge than Lexington.

"That's due to the angels." Alex exhaled. "We all hate to admit it, but the buildings are made with materials they brought from Heaven."

That explained how the glass seemed more vibrant than any I'd ever seen before and the lines extra precise. "Heaven." That sounded so weird to say. I hadn't grown up a believer, but now I knew angels were real. "Does Satan exist too?" If I was going to run into Satan, I wanted a warning.

"Not exactly." He snorted. "The angels here didn't agree with how Heaven was overseen, so they came to Earth to live. They brought materials with them to make their new home more comfortable for them."

I wanted to ask more, but my brain had already maxed out. I had a feeling if I got him too far down the path of details, he might talk my head off for years.

Griffin turned left, but we continued straight on, going deeper into the city. "Why aren't we following them?"

"Because they're going to their home, and we're going to ours." He continued to drive slowly through the city.

No one paid attention to us. Half the people were dressed in jeans and shirts, while the other half looked like they were out for a night on the town. Groups of friends converged. Others walked past without acknowledging anyone outside their group.

A white building, which reminded me of the Capitol Building outside Shadow City, came into view on our left. It appeared different from the taller buildings, and its rectangular shape, with a tower on top, covered an entire block. A parking lot sat beside it, the only designated parking I'd seen since we entered the city. "That sticks out."

"That's the council building." Alex's grip tightened on the steering wheel, his knuckles white. "Every council member can come and go in Shadow City, and they opted to tear down a building to make a parking lot for members with vehicles."

"Gotcha. But why make the building look like human architecture?"

"To remind everyone that the council has pure intentions," Alex deadpanned. "The most corrupt angel, Azbogah, demanded that the building be designed like this."

The people with the most to hide often made sure they appeared self-righteous. "Like making the building different from the rest of the city would keep people from questioning the council's decision? That makes no sense." It was human nature to question things, and I assumed that also was true for supernaturals.

"It doesn't, but it's true that no one questions us." Alex tapped a finger on the steering wheel. "Because the council hurts those who do, which means we have to be *really* careful when it comes to you."

The conversation back at Sterlyn's had made the situation seem a little promising. "I thought we had the majority vote."

"We do, and that'll make the members who are against you being here even more dangerous." He glanced at me. "Some members will want to hurt you to get their way. It happened to Sterlyn."

"Really?" I couldn't imagine anyone not liking her. She was the sincerest person I'd ever met. "But they worked through it."

"It took killing a council member and his mate while imprisoning their daughter to get there." Alex's jaw twitched. "It wasn't easy."

"But you helped them, right?"

"Oh, I did." His face hardened. "But I helped them, so they'd owe me. Remember the favor I cashed in for you to stay with them? That was from when all that stuff was going on."

"Hey." I placed my hand on his arm. "You can't change what you did in the past. All you can do is move forward and be a better person." Eliza had told me that over and over, and I clung to that belief. Hearing his story reinforced that she'd been right.

The buildings grew larger, but they were built more like condominiums and apartment buildings instead of businesses. We'd driven through the city center and were approaching the outer wall.

Alex slowed and pointed at a four-story Neo-Renaissance-style building with a regal air, shining in the moonlight. "Home sweet home."

"Wow." I'd figured they'd have a big house, but I hadn't expected *this*. "It's huge."

"Over eight-thousand-square feet, and sometimes it still feels small with Matthew and Gwen living here too." Alex grimaced. "With all of us close by, you will be better protected."

He turned down the drive, pulled up to the far end of the house, and pressed a garage door opener on the visor. I couldn't even see a door until a section of the building lifted; it was so well camouflaged with the house.

As we pulled in, I scanned the interior. The garage floor was dark gray tile, and lantern-like lights hung from the ceiling every five feet. Bulky red columns marked parking spots for each car, and Alex drove by a Lexus SUV and a Porsche before parking in the spot closest to a cherrywood door.

"I get that you're a prince, but do you guys need all this?" For some reason, I didn't expect them to be able to afford all of this since they'd been closed off in this city for one thousand years. That prince was more of a courtly title, but they had the money to back up their royal status. "If this is the garage, I can't imagine what the house looks like inside."

"Lucky for you, we have the whole top floor to ourselves." He put the car in park and winked. "Matthew has to stay on the bottom floor for security reasons, but because I'm the spare, I got to choose which floor would be mine after my parents died. I took the top one for its access to the rooftop balcony."

That sounded nice. "We'll have to check that out."

"We definitely will." He opened his door and reached into the back to grab my bag.

Desperate to see the inside, I jumped out of the car and headed to the door to the house. It opened into an enormous foyer with marble floors and canary yellow walls. My attention went to an oversized chandelier hanging in the center. It reminded me of a peacock.

Someone inhaled, and my attention flicked to a man across the room in a black suit, his cedar hair perfectly slicked back and styled. His body stiffened, and his ever-green eyes turned crimson as his fangs jutted from his mouth.

I stumbled backward to return to the garage and Alex, but that had been the wrong move. The man blurred, coming right at me.

CHAPTER EIGHT

I screamed, and the man landed on me. I fell to the floor on my back. A sickening crack sounded, and immense pain exploded in my head. My vision hazed over as the man went for my neck.

The door swung open, and the man disappeared from on top of me. I grabbed my neck as nausea churned in my stomach. I needed to make sure he hadn't severed my artery, but I didn't feel a drop of moisture.

He hadn't bitten me.

"Do *not* touch her again," Alex seethed.

Again, he'd saved me from becoming someone's meal. This was turning into a theme between us.

"I...I'm sorry," the man rasped. "It's just, I've never smelled someone so irresistible before. I—"

Ugh, my head hurt so damn bad, and I was frustrated that I hadn't even considered that. If most of the vampires living in the city had remained isolated here, they'd never been tempted by a human before. And here I'd come, waltzing in as if I didn't have a care in the world. I was so stupid.

Footsteps hurried into the room, and Matthew hissed, "Alex, what are you doing?"

Cool hands brushed my hair from my face, and Gwen leaned over me, her face etched with concern. "Where does it hurt?"

"The back of my head." If it hadn't hurt so damn bad, I'd have been embarrassed, but I couldn't get there right now. I forced my head to turn and found Alex with his hands wrapped around my attacker's neck, pressing him against the wall. The room spun, making it hard to focus on them.

I closed my eyes, needing relief, but it didn't come. My entire body spun as if I were on a fast-moving carousel. "I might puke."

"Alex, help your mate," Matthew said. "I'll handle Sergio."

"He tried to feed off her," Alex growled.

Sergio's voice shook as he said, "My prince, I didn't mean to. It was an accident, and I had no clue she was your mate. She just smells so good."

"This is going to be a problem with any vampire who hasn't ventured out of the city," Matthew said curtly. "Something else you should've considered before completing the bond with her."

He was right, but this guy appeared ashamed of his actions. Regret wafted off him. I needed to get Alex over here before he did something we'd both regret. *I need you.*

The moment I thought those words, he released his hold on Sergio's neck and stepped backward toward me. He rasped, "Can I trust you to keep it together?"

"Yes. I'll never attack her again." Sergio lifted his hands. "I swear it."

"Go on." Matthew rubbed the back of his neck. "I'll make sure nothing happens."

Alex huffed. "And that should make me feel better?"

Matthew crossed his arms and frowned. "I'll pretend I didn't hear that."

The spinning slowed down, but I couldn't get my bearings. I'd never liked amusement parks.

"Your pupils are dilated." Gwen placed her hand on my forehead. "Drinking some vampire blood would make you feel better."

Yeah, I didn't want to do that in front of everyone, and I didn't want to drink anyone's blood but Alex's. The thought of drinking blood from him again sounded appealing, but not enough to do it now. "Nah, I'm good."

I rolled to my side and pushed myself up, determined to sit, but I almost toppled over. Strong, familiar arms wrapped around me, preventing me from hitting the floor.

"Not too fast," Alex scolded.

Normally, that would have annoyed me, but feeling the way I did, safe in his arms, it didn't. He could lecture me all he wanted as long as he stayed right here beside me. *I don't think he meant to hurt me. He seemed surprised when I entered the room and stared at me for a second. He only sprang at me when I moved to go back into the garage.*

He was probably fighting it, then you acted like prey. Alex exhaled and shifted his arm.

I groaned in protest until his fingers gently moved my hair to the side so he could examine the wound. When he touched the spot, I grimaced. "Ow."

"Sorry." He lifted his hand to his mouth. *Here, take a few sips of my blood. It'll make you feel better.* He held his wrist to my mouth. It had two bite marks where he'd pierced his skin. Blood trickled down his forearm. *You won't need much, and you'll heal faster.*

I shook my head. *Uh...your siblings and Sergio are around.* I had to draw boundaries somewhere.

I moved my legs to stand, but when I put weight down, the room swirled faster than before. I was going to vomit in front of everyone. *Fine.* I sat again and leaned my back against his chest. *I'll do it.*

Yeah, I figured you might change your mind. He chuckled and held his wrist out to me again.

Feeling self-conscious, I touched the tip of my tongue to the blood. I closed my mouth as the delicious syrup taste filled it, soothing my stomach immediately. The pain in my head receded, and I couldn't believe how much better I felt in just seconds.

"Was it that bad?" Gwen smiled sadly as she examined my face again. "Your pupils are back to normal. If you drink more—"

It felt way too sensual to be doing that in front of everyone, and even though I'd craved his blood while we'd been intimate, I didn't so much right now. My human side was fully intact, even if his blood tasted like candy.

"Miss." Sergio adjusted his white button-down shirt and straightened his tie. "I really am sorry. That will never happen again."

"Damn straight it won't," Alex said. "Because if it does, I will kill you myself."

I turned my head and kissed Alex's cheek. Although I thoroughly enjoyed his broody protectiveness, this poor guy had beaten himself up enough. "I can't say it's okay because I was scared for my life." I tried to joke, but it fell flat. Probably too soon for death jokes. "But I believe you, and I forgive you."

"Thank you." He moved toward me then stopped short. "But I think it's wise that I keep my distance. You smell very appealing."

A shiver ran down my spine. If anyone but a vampire had informed me of that, I'd have been flattered, but I'd rather smell like garbage to him. "Uh...is there a way I can help with that?" I racked my brain for things that vampires didn't like. "Perhaps I should eat a lot of garlic?"

"That won't help." Matthew glared at me. "If you knew anything about supernaturals, you wouldn't be making such stereotypical comments."

Wow. And here I was hoping that Matthew and I could get to know each other and become amicable during my time here. I was beginning to think that wouldn't happen.

"Stop acting like a prick." Alex stood and helped me

to my feet. "She can't help that she was born human, just like we can't help that we were born vampires."

"But because we're vampires, we live here." Matthew faced us, his hands fisted at his sides. "She's human and shouldn't be anywhere near us."

"There are humans all over Shadow Terrace." I couldn't let Alex fight my battles for me, and if I wanted Matthew to respect me, I had to stand my ground. "So your statement doesn't fully stack up. You need human blood to survive. Whether you like it or not, vampires and humans are linked."

Gwen laughed. "She's got you there, brother."

"Not funny." Matthew sneered at her. "You aren't helping matters."

"You've said your piece, and you wanted us to stay here." Alex wrapped an arm around my waist. "You can't influence us to come here then act like you don't want her here."

I kept driving a wedge between Alex and his brother. Now I'd added Gwen to the equation, but I wasn't willing to give Alex up, not anymore.

I was encouraged that his sister was warming up to me. Maybe there was hope for me and Matthew after all.

"Because you're my brother and need to be here." Matthew rocked on his heels. "It's not like I had much of a choice."

"Then you'd better start accepting this." Alex scowled at Sergio and Matthew. "I'm taking Veronica to our room. Please inform the other staff that there is a human on the premises, and this is now her permanent home. If anything happens to her, I'll kill them myself."

I tried to connect with Alex, but our connection was on the fritz. I could only guess that it was another problem created by my human side. We could only connect well when I was highly emotional.

Alex led me to a towering marble staircase in the middle of the room. He bent and lifted me into his arms then hurried up the stairs. I glanced over his shoulder to find Matthew glaring at me with so much hatred my breath hitched. I didn't know what I'd done to deserve so much malice.

I heard the rustling of the bag being lifted off the floor, and Gwen's voice sounded as if she was getting closer to the stairs. "You told me you would warn everyone that a human was coming. What the hell happened?"

"Business came up, and I didn't get around to it," Matthew answered, as if it wasn't a big deal.

She grunted. "Not a good reason. She's family now." Climbing the stairs, she called back, "Sergio, please inform everyone about Veronica so no one makes the same mistake you did."

"Yes, Your Royal Highness," Sergio replied.

Alex stepped onto a small landing that connected to another staircase. A hallway off the landing was twenty feet wide with dark wooden walls and another chandelier, this one reminding me of a waterfall. The same marble floor ran down the hall.

As Alex turned to continue up the stairs, I patted his shoulder. "You know I can walk, right?"

"Not chancing it." He continued without pausing. "You took hardly any blood, and you hit your head hard. Between that and the earlier attack, I won't risk you getting injured again."

The adrenaline from the day was wearing off, and my eyelids were growing heavy. "Your sister is following us with our bag."

"I wanted her to," he confided. "Something is going on with my brother, and I don't like it. I want to talk with her about it."

Yeah, I'd gotten the same vibe. "He doesn't like me."

"He doesn't like change." We reached another landing and continued around to the next staircase. This floor was identical with a different chandelier reminding me of fireworks. "It's nothing personal."

Maybe not...but I wasn't buying it. In the middle of the long hallway, near a bank of windows, sat a black grand piano. On the wall next to it was a painting of what had to be younger versions of Matthew, Alex, and Gwen with two people standing behind them whom Alex resembled perfectly. A small smile spread across my face at the image, but I was too tired to ask about it. I leaned my head on Alex's chest and drifted off before he reached the top of the stairs.

"Good morning, Princess," Gwen said, waking me from my sleep.

I blinked my eyes open and glanced around a huge, unfamiliar room. The entire wall to the right was glass with shimmery blinds letting light shine through. The other walls were a charcoal gray, sleek and modern. To my left was a large painting of the city skyline, reminding me of the city emblem, with two towering buildings right in the center and smaller ones on both sides. I sat up and found myself in a gigantic bed. Muted gray sheets and a puffy comforter that felt like a cloud surrounded me, and a sizable, fluffy pillow bore my head imprint.

Pushing the covers off me, I reached into my back pocket and damn near cried in relief when I felt my phone. I quickly unlocked it and found an unread text from Annie.

Thank goodness. Relief washed over me now that she was home.

Hey, I'm home. Eliza is upset that you aren't with me, so don't be surprised if you hear from her soon. I love you and already miss you. See you soon. XO

I typed out a reply:

Thanks for letting me know. I miss you too. Talk very soon. I love you.

I pressed send then tossed the phone on the bed and gazed at Gwen. "Is this Alex's room?"

"Technically, the room belongs to the both of you now." Gwen smiled as she placed a modest black skirt and a sky-blue blouse on the bed. "I figured blue would look great with your copper hair."

"Wait." My mind was foggy, probably from everything that had happened yesterday. "Is this for the emergency council meeting Alex and the others are expecting?"

"Yup. Being presentable and modest is the best way to go—for you, anyway." She rubbed a hand down her short, crimson sundress, which fit perfectly. "Since they're used to seeing me dress this way, I'll keep to my usual fashion."

Even if they hadn't been, I had a feeling she'd do whatever the hell she wanted. "Yeah, good idea." I glanced at the clothes, surprised because I would've picked them out for myself. "Do you, by chance, have shoes I can wear?"

"Of course." She pointed down at the charcoal carpet.

I leaned forward to see modest black dress shoes with two-inch heels at my feet. "Well, okay then. Where is your brother?"

"Talking to Matthew and finding you something to eat." She gestured to the door behind her. "Hurry up and get dressed. Matthew and I are leaving to head to the council building, and you and Alex need to follow right behind. Once I shut the door, don't open it for anyone but Alex."

"Uh...yeah." I could do that. I didn't want a repeat performance of last night. "Got it."

"And make sure you act confident and comfortable around everyone." She strolled to the door and opened it. "That's the only way the council members will believe you can survive in this world. One sign of hesitation is all it will take to make everyone doubt you." She shut the door behind her, leaving me alone to process her words.

No pressure.

I jumped to my feet and quickly changed into the dress clothes. I didn't want to be the reason we ran late. I already had too much to prove without adding *lack of punctuality* to my list of faults.

In seconds, I had my outfit on. I rushed into the bathroom, hoping to find a hairbrush and toothbrush. The entire bathroom was charcoal-gray tile with a white marble floor. The wide double vanity matched the walls. Sitting between the two sinks were the toiletries I needed.

Alex had taken care of me again.

As I brushed my hair and then my teeth, I scanned the rest of the bathroom. The massive rain shower was made of the same marble as the floor, and the toilet sat between the shower and the wall. The bathroom was maybe a quarter of the size of the bedroom.

Once I was ready, I stared in the mirror. My green eyes appeared light and sparkly, and my copper hair seemed glossier than usual. It totally had to be the lighting.

I didn't have any makeup, so my natural look would have to do.

In the mirror, the shadow appeared beside me. A scream lodged in my throat, but I was too frozen in fear to get it out. I turned my head to find myself face to face with it. Its eyes glowed a faint green, and something buzzed under my skin.

My body shook. It was doing something to me. I tried to break free, but it was like I was paralyzed.

It lifted a hand to me, the way it had when I'd been in danger.

CHAPTER NINE

The shadow's hand touched my cheek, and something inside me shifted. My pulse calmed, and my breathing evened out. I was no longer petrified, which freaked me out. Its touch felt familiar.

The familiarity had to be from when it had helped me stab Zaro. It had grabbed my hand, controlling me, so I could kill the vampire. In that moment, I hadn't been paying attention, too focused on not dying.

No, I couldn't get comfortable with this monster. It had tormented me for the first fourteen years of my life before I'd found Eliza and Annie. Since then, I hadn't seen the shadow until I'd gotten here.

That couldn't be coincidental.

Maybe this was a supernatural creature haunting me. That would make sense.

I reached up to push the hand away...and my hand went through the appendage. I froze.

The shadow cupped my face, and cold spread across my cheek. I sensed it was trying to warn me. I leaned into its touch and marveled at its solidity.

Holy shit, there was no getting out of this.

A faint knock, followed by a click of the lock and the bedroom door opening, pulled me back to the present. "Veronica?" Alex called.

"In here." My voice shook, conveying my apprehension. No one had ever seen the shadow, so I wasn't worried that Alex was at risk. Maybe he could make it disappear.

Alex blurred into the room as the shadow vanished. He materialized right where the shadow had been.

"What's wrong?" He examined our surroundings. "Was someone in here?"

"Not exactly." The last time I'd told someone about the shadow, they'd threaten to lock me up. I'd never mentioned it again, not even to Eliza. But it had returned, and I didn't know what to do.

His forehead lined with worry. "What do you mean?"

I blew out a breath. "I...I don't know." My mind raced over how to explain the crazy occurrences that were becoming the norm in my world.

"You can tell me anything." He took my hand, still glancing around to determine what had happened.

He was my mate, so he was stuck with me, crazy and all. Maybe letting someone in on this secret would make it better. "I haven't even discussed this with Eliza."

His eyebrows arched. "Really?" He rubbed his thumb against my hand. "This admission would normally exhilarate me, but the expression on your face makes me wish there was nothing to share."

I had to get it out there. The longer I debated what to say and how to say it, the more difficult it would be to say it. "I see a shadow."

"A shadow?" His voice was tense. "I'm assuming you don't mean the kind made by the sun, moon, and lights?"

That was a very interesting way to word the question. "No. It can materialize even in the dark, and it hovers over me."

His body stilled. "How long has that been happening?"

"For as long as I can remember." This sounded insane. "But the morning they took me to Eliza's was the last time I saw it. I have no clue why, and I've never questioned it. I was just grateful that the shadow was gone."

"And you're just telling me about this now?" Anger tinged his words.

No, he didn't get to be an asshole. "Yes—because it left for several years and only came back in Shadow Terrace. At first, I thought I was seeing things, but it's real. It appears when I'm in danger. It appeared the first night I came to Shadow Terrace, right before Klyn attacked me, and it helped me that night at the blood bank."

"What do you mean exactly?"

"When Zaro attacked me, the shadow laid on top of

me and helped me stab him." Okay, saying it out loud sounded even crazier.

His jaw twitched, and his eyes turned navy. "And did you see it just now?"

"Yeah." I didn't see any point in hiding the truth. "It was right where you're standing. It...touched my cheek." I might as well just tell him everything. "And its touch felt familiar. But that familiarity probably stems from it helping me kill Zaro, right?"

"I have no clue." Alex pinched the bridge of his nose. "Your emotions slammed into me downstairs, and I sensed a mixture of concern and discomfort. I thought it was because we're heading to the council meeting, but I rushed up here to see what was wrong." He kissed my forehead. "I'm glad I did."

"Me too." I leaned into his chest and sighed as he wrapped his arms around me. "It vanished once you got here. Do you have any idea what it could be?"

"I have a few guesses." He dropped his arms and stepped back. "Are you okay to go? We need to head to the meeting, but I don't want to drag you there before you're ready."

"We can't be late." I'd dealt with the shadow most of my life and couldn't let this latest incident hinder me.

He nodded. "Yes, but your health is more important to me."

"Even if it's mental?" I tried to tease, but again, my joke fell flat. I had to get better at joking during serious moments. Sierra made it look so easy.

"Especially if it's mental." He winked, his arrogance making me feel more grounded. He was acting like himself, which was exactly what I needed. "But your body is important as well." He perused my figure, and heat flashed through me.

"If you keep that up, we won't be getting anywhere on time." I inhaled deeply, determined to keep my shit together. "Let's go, but I want to hear your theories on the way. I always thought I was losing my mind whenever I'd see it."

"I'll tell you anything you want." He intertwined our fingers and led me out of the bedroom.

In the hallway, my breathing hitched. Several paintings of the two older people I'd seen in the family photo decorated the walls. Alex cherished his family, and that was one of the many things I loved about him. "Are those your parents?"

"Yes." He smiled sadly. "I wish you could've met them."

"Me too." And I surprised myself by truly meaning it. Tearing my gaze away, I surveyed the rest of the hallway. I didn't remember Alex carrying me up here, but it had the same layout as the other floors I'd seen. I remembered my less-than-ideal introduction to the household. "Is Sergio okay?"

"Yes." Alex walked a few steps ahead of me, acting like my protector again. "But I don't want to take any chances. A few of the vampire staff were talking about how good Sergio said you smell. I don't want you going anywhere without me by your side until they get more comfortable with you."

Part of me wanted to push the conversation and hear his guesses about the shadow, but I could wait until we got outside. I didn't want to distract him when he was protecting me from being eaten.

Words I'd never thought would cross my mind. That was how much my life had changed in my time here.

Until Sergio had attacked me, I hadn't considered that vampires might have a hard time controlling themselves around me. But it made sense. Whenever I went into a bakery and smelled fresh cinnamon rolls, drool always collected in my mouth, and I could never deny myself the pleasure of eating one. For vampires to suddenly have the equivalent of a decadent dessert standing in front of them had to be hard to resist.

On the bottom floor, two beautiful women with long, warm-brown hair were cleaning the windows. I could tell the moment they smelled me because their arms stilled, and they turned to me in unison.

Their fangs extended from their mouths, and red filled their already amber eyes. Their chests heaved, and they dropped the rags from their hands.

It reminded me of a horror movie. The two of them were twins, and their matching outfits—black dresses that resembled the style of Sergio's clothing from last night—made the feeling more over the top.

They stepped toward me, and Alex blocked them. "Back off," he hissed. "This is your new princess."

But it was like they didn't comprehend his words.

"Dammit." He growled, spun around, and lifted me.

He took off toward the door to the garage, and I heard the two women running after us.

It seemed like every time I turned around, I was putting Alex in the awful position of protecting me. I hated to be a nuisance, especially when I needed to prove I could stand beside him, but I obviously couldn't. My mere presence in the city drove vampires crazy with bloodlust. Maybe that had been Matthew's motive for pushing us to come here—so he could prove I wasn't meant to live in their world.

That both irritated me and made me respect him. Instead of pushing Alex to leave me behind, he'd commanded him to bring me here, knowing that shit like this would ensue.

The world blurred as Alex ran, but I could hear the other two gaining on us. When we got to the door, he'd have to pause to open it, giving them a chance to catch us.

"Stop!" Sergio called as his figure blurred between us and the two women. "You need to get your heads together."

The three blurry shapes collided.

"No!" I didn't want Sergio to get hurt either.

The three of them came back into view as Alex reached the door and threw it open. Sergio held each woman by the neck, lifting them up and keeping them from following. He turned to me, his teeth extended and his irises crimson, before he grimaced in discomfort.

As the door shut, I said, "Thank you," knowing his supernatural hearing would pick up my words.

In the garage, Alex slowed and stopped at the car. He unlocked and opened the passenger door and placed me inside.

Within seconds, he'd shut my door and climbed in behind the steering wheel. He sat for a second and exhaled, running a hand down his face. "Veronica, I'm so sorry."

"For what?" He had nothing to apologize for. This wasn't his doing, and it wasn't the vampires' fault either. They hadn't grown up needing to fight their cravings.

He held his hands in front of him. "Danger keeps finding you."

"Thanks to you." I touched his arm.

"Not sure you should be thanking me." His shoulders sagged in defeat.

Yeah, that hadn't come out like I'd meant it to. "No, I mean because of you, I'm alive to be put in more danger." Yeah, none of that sounded the way I'd wanted it to.

He chuckled sadly. "That's true, but I'm not sure that makes it better."

"I thought we were walking." He'd commented that the parking lot was for people who traveled into the city from the outside world.

He started the car. "This is the vampire part of the city, and I won't expose you on the sidewalk. We will be driving. You should be relatively safe once we arrive. The council building is located closer to the shifter and angel neighborhoods."

Good to know. "On our way there, I'd love to learn more about the city."

"Yes, it would be good if you went into the council meeting knowing more about the supernatural races." He opened the garage door and pulled out of the parking spot.

As we drove into the daylight, I blinked. I hadn't expected what I saw. The light was full of beautiful colors like a kaleidoscope. Pinks, blues, purples, and oranges flickered constantly, creating the impression that we had entered a different realm. "It's beautiful."

"Oh, yeah." He grinned. "The dome causes it. Apparently, Heaven looks like this."

Of course, it did. I leaned forward to view the glass dome over the city, and it was even more breathtaking. But we had things to go over. "Tell me your ideas about the shadow."

"My first guess is that maybe someone in your family pissed off a witch, and it's some sort of spell. Witches are super powerful when they work together, and they could have created a nearly sentient shadow." He turned onto the road that led through the city.

My mind churned. "If they're powerful, then the shadow wouldn't have disappeared, would it?"

"Their strength is also their weakness. Something as simple as one caster becoming ill, or turning against their practices or mission, can fracture their power, which could be why the shadow disappeared." He fidgeted in his seat. "If that person recovered or was replaced, or if they left the coven or died, the spell could be cast again."

"I've sensed the shadow my entire life, though. Why

would witches be tormenting me?" I hadn't done anything to anyone that I knew of.

He watched me. "It could be a grudge passed down to you from a family member. What do you know about your blood family?"

"Nothing." I hated being clueless. "My mother died in a car wreck while she was pregnant with me, and since she had no living relatives, I became a ward of the state." In my mind, I always pictured my mom as a good person and carefree, but I didn't have any information to back that up. What if she'd been a horrible person? "Do you think she was a witch?"

"No. You don't smell like a witch." He tapped his nose. "I'd know, and you'd be a quarter witch at least, which you couldn't hide. It's easy to anger a witch, though."

"Any other guesses?" I turned to him, enjoying his strong neckline. He was ruggedly regal, which I never would've believed was my type. I couldn't imagine anyone even half as handsome and caring as him.

"I've also heard that a demon can hide within shadows, but you can actually see this shadow. Demons can't project like witches can. It would have to be physically around you." He focused on the road as the white building came into view. "And from what my father told us centuries ago, the demons and angels have a truce. Demons don't come to Shadow City as long as we don't interfere with them, so for the shadow to be in the city, my bet is on the source being a witch."

I wasn't sure if I'd rather it be a demon or a witch's spell. They both sounded scary. "How so?"

"The powerful magic that protects the city should block out witch magic unless a spell is being cast by someone inside." He turned into the lot on the right side of the council building. "Which means we have to figure out who the hell it is before things get worse. Your arrival in Shadow Terrace sounds like it escalated things with the shadow, but I don't see how anyone from Shadow City could be connected to your family unless the connection is from generations ago."

"Could a witch have killed my mom?" Could my family have been cursed before Shadow City was created?

Rosemary stood in front of the building and rushed toward us as her flowy burnt-orange shirt billowed behind her.

His mood somber, Alex turned off the car. "That is a possibility. We need to pay special attention to the three witch representatives. Maybe they will give us a clue."

My door opened, and Rosemary scowled at Alex. "Mom and Dad alerted me of a huge problem from the council room."

I'd forgotten until this moment that both of Rosemary's parents were part of the council.

"What now?" Alex asked.

"Your brother is in there whispering to the witches and Azbogah." She glanced at me. "He's trying to get them to agree to let her live here only if she's turned."

"Turned?" No. That couldn't mean what I thought it did.

"That's why he rushed to get here early." Alex's nostrils flared as pink bled into his irises. "He wasn't helping me. He wants to force my hand to either turn Veronica into one of us or send her home."

My vision darkened. I loved Alex, but could I give up my human life for him? I wasn't so sure.

CHAPTER TEN

R osemary opened the door wider and gestured for me to get out. "We need to get in there before Matthew sways them to his side."

My mind was reeling. I'd thought Matthew would have talked to me before trying to force my hand since I was his brother's soul mate. I assumed that he would at least be a little respectful. I'd never imagined that Alex turning me was a possibility, likely because we'd been dealing with one emergency after another. I couldn't believe I hadn't considered it before.

The two of them continued to talk, but I couldn't make out their words as my internal struggle increased. I followed them on autopilot and contemplated how I felt. If I didn't turn, I'd grow old while Alex remained the same. I'd get wrinkled and gray, and he'd still look twenty and in tip-top shape. which didn't sound ideal.

And I would die. What would happen to Alex then?

Why couldn't I stay human and become ageless?

That was the best solution but obviously not an option. I wasn't even sure how someone was turned. If I had to choose, I wasn't sure which way to go. Becoming a vampire made me a threat to Annie and Eliza because I'd be thirsting for their blood, but staying human meant I would grow old and die. Neither option was great.

"Veronica," Alex said, squeezing my arm gently to pull me back to the present. "Are you okay?"

"Define 'okay.'" I hadn't been okay since...well, forever. I'd grown up without parents and always had the shadow hanging around. The only time I'd been fine was while living with Eliza and Annie, but now that I'd met Alex, that wasn't true anymore.

Meeting Alex was the best thing that had ever happened to me.

"I will say things are never dull around here." Rosemary shook her head. "Since Atticus died, the corruption and politics around Shadow City have been like a runaway train barely staying on the tracks."

"Griffin's father was a great man, but many of these issues started before his death," Alex said as we walked up to a huge hunter-green door that led inside. "It just snowballed from there, especially since Sterlyn showed up."

Rosemary nodded. "Azbogah is the main proponent of not having a silver wolf involved in any way, and we both know he's in deep with Erin and getting his claws into your brother. I'm sure Matthew got the idea to turn Ronnie from him."

We entered a massive and mostly bare entry hall, the

once-white walls stained light yellow from time and wear. A tall, pale man wearing a loose black outfit was sweeping the spotless marble floor. I had no clue what he was cleaning, but he worked methodically.

The scent of coffee hit my nose, and my gaze flicked to a small coffee stand built into a corner of the room. There wasn't a table, not even for creamer.

As the door shut behind us, the wind pushed past me, and the man with the broom froze. His head snapped to me, and his fangs extended as his eyes took on a red hue.

"Get her inside the council room," Rosemary commanded. She stepped in front of me as the vampire barreled toward us. "I'll take care of him as silently as possible."

Alex tugged me toward the only other door inside the building, another hunter-green entry, and Rosemary punched the vampire in the face, knocking him down.

The faint stench of decay hit me, and my stomach heaved. "Why does he stink so bad?" I was used to vampires smelling sweet like syrup, cotton candy, chocolate ice cream, or ripe fruit. This vampire smelled like death.

"He's being starved as punishment." Alex opened the door, placed his hand on the small of my back, and guided me inside. "So, he's even hungrier than our staff at the mansion."

In other words, another supernatural that couldn't control themselves around me.

The room we entered was dominated by a long rectangular table with a cut-out section that faced the door.

Eleven people sat at the far side of the table, watching us enter. I wondered which ones were the witches.

Feeling under scrutiny, I glanced to my left. Two empty chairs sat against the freshly painted white wall.

My fears about being intimidated had been justified because the only person who looked at me with a smile was Sterlyn. She sat between Matthew and a man who towered over everyone, even though he was seated.

His wintery-gray eyes locked on me, and he snarled, "This is the human causing all the problems?" His spiked caramel hair and midnight black wings made his stoic expression more cutting. His black suit, similar to Matthew's, added to his commanding presence, but something dark hovered over him.

"Yes, that's her, Azbogah." Matthew leaned forward to peer around Sterlyn at the dark angel. "She partly caused this mess."

He'd pretty much informed everyone here—including me—that he didn't like me. I'd hoped we could tolerate each other for Alex's sake.

Sterlyn cut her eyes at the vampire king. "That's not true, and you know it. There are circumstances that the council should know about."

Alex tensed beside me, and I realized what she meant. The council wasn't aware that vampires were feeding on and killing humans. They thought the vampires were supposed to protect this hidden city, but they didn't know about the rogues that had lost their humanity, leading them to engage in criminal activity.

"What is she talking about?" A shorter woman pushed her black and scarlet-streaked hair behind her shoulders. "What do we not know?" She squinted her misty gray eyes surrounded by thick black eyeliner. Something about her made me think she couldn't be trusted.

"Nothing, Erin," Matthew spat, glaring at Sterlyn. "She's trying to cause problems."

I'd opened my mouth to say something when a woman with full blood-red lips sitting on the left side of the long table clicked her tongue, studying me with forest-green eyes that were bright with interest. "Sterlyn doesn't cause problems for fun, so I find that hard to believe, especially with you acting guilty." She wore a black dress so tight it could've been a second skin, and her black wings blended in with the material. The dark colors made her amber hair shine brightly. A faint glow, one similar to Sterlyn's, emanated from within her. She was absolutely breathtaking.

"I agree with Yelahiah," Griffin growled. "And, insult my mate one more time, and we'll see who's the one causing problems." He sat near one end of the table, next to Yelahiah and an empty seat, allowing him to glare at Matthew.

Panic wafted through me. This council was divided. I'd gathered some tension was to be expected, but this was worse than I'd imagined.

"Oh, please." A young woman with long burgundy hair shifted in the seat closest to us. She rolled her eyes and crossed her arms. "Don't act all cocky. We all know any supernatural outside of our coven can't be trusted."

"That's enough, Diana." A thin man leaned forward in his chair directly across from the girl. His wings spread behind him, the feathers a purer white than his suit. The only colors on him were the butterscotch blond of his hair and the piercing sky blue of his eyes. "We are supposed to be working together, not insulting one another. That goes for everyone."

"I'm with Pahaliah," a young woman with waist-length, dark brown hair said. She leaned back in her chair, almost brushing elbows with Matthew and Yelahiah. She nibbled on her black-stained lip while her coffee-colored eyes stared at the table.

"Shut up, Breena," Erin hissed. "I speak on behalf of the coven, not you." A vileness wafted off the woman. I sensed she was capable of horrible acts, including killing someone and haunting another in any way she could.

The races were divided within themselves. Alex's theory about the shadow strengthened in my mind. Maybe with my closer proximity, conjuring the shadow took less magic and that was why it had reappeared.

"You realize that's not how this council works?" The handsome young man sitting between Gwen and Pahaliah chuckled. Sea-green eyes, which contrasted with his olive skin, sparkled with interest. "If it was, then Griffin and Sterlyn would make decisions for the wolves and other shifters, but instead, they listen to what I have to say and don't bully me into voting the way they want me to." He ran a hand through brown-sable hair that fell naturally around his face.

"Oh, yes." Matthew glowered. "We can't forget how *amazing* Sterlyn and Griffin are."

"Someone sounds jealous." Alex laughed and wrapped an arm around my waist. "Is that how I used to sound?" he asked, glancing at Yelahiah then Gwen.

"Yes," Yelahiah responded with a bluntness that was so characteristically Rosemary. That was obviously a family trait...or maybe an angel one. Regardless, I found the quality very endearing.

Matthew slammed his hand on the table. "Now listen—"

"We didn't come here to bicker," Sterlyn jumped in, power radiating off her. It was clear she was meant to be part of this council. "We came here to discuss allowing a human to enter Shadow City."

"Yes, a decision made by you, your mate, and Alex." Erin wrinkled her nose. "Not by the council as a whole."

"She's here because my dear brother—the king of the vampires—demanded that Veronica stay with me in our mansion." Alex had thrown his brother under the bus. "Four of the twelve members of the council, which is a third of us, made the decision. The Divine states that in a new situation, a third can pass a temporary decision until the full council can convene."

"Is that right?" Azbogah arched an eyebrow at Matthew.

Gwen cleared her throat. "Five including me, dear

brother. Don't forget I wanted her with us as well. So, it was over the minimum one-third required."

No, she hadn't. But both she and Alex knew that Matthew was forcing their hand, and if I was going to be part of their world, they had to agree. I doubted they'd realized what the consequences of bringing me here would be until Sergio had attacked me. However, Gwen had sided with Alex and me, and that made me feel more connected to her.

"You can see we followed protocol." Matthew smiled smugly, looking ecstatic that his brother and sister had backed him, but I had a feeling they'd done it to protect me more than anything else. "But in less than twenty-four hours, her presence has caused several issues, including our butler, who has been in our service for over two hundred years, attacking her on sight."

The door behind us opened, and Rosemary entered the room. She tugged the hem of her shirt over her black slacks as she came to stand beside me.

Alex had explained that Rosemary was next in line to be part of the council, so she could attend all the meetings to prepare for her future role in case something happened to either one of her parents.

"That's what I was afraid of." Azbogah *tsked* and frowned while mirth danced behind his eyes. He'd enjoyed learning that information. "Most of the Shadow City vampires haven't learned how to control their urges because a human has never been in the city before. We can't jeopardize their mental wellness over one human who wants to be part of our society."

Erin nodded. "Even though witches are the closest to human among all the races, our magic enhances our blood, so it is poison to vampires, and they are not tempted to drink from us. It makes sense that she needs to leave or be turned."

"How does a human even get turned?" The question had been bubbling in the back of my mind since Rosemary had met us outside.

"You haven't told her anything, have you?" Erin smirked at Alex. "A vampire bites you and injects you with their poison."

"She didn't need to know because it's not happening," Alex said loudly. "She is my soulmate, and she shouldn't be punished for it."

My face heated, and I blinked back sudden tears. His words hurt. Even though I wasn't sure whether I wanted to be turned, my heart had reacted instantly to Alex's opposition to the idea. How would we have a future otherwise?

"Wait." Yelahiah stood, her head tilted toward me. "No one said she was your soulmate." She scanned me, and I felt more like a science experiment than a person. Something unreadable crossed her face.

"It doesn't matter if she's his soulmate." Azbogah scoffed and waved a hand at me. "She's human and a threat to our way of life."

"And she knows too much." Erin patted the table with her hand. "I vote that she leaves and gets her mind wiped by a vampire."

I hated to be discussed as if I wasn't in the room, and

there was no way in hell I was leaving Alex behind. "They can't erase my memory. Alex has already tried."

Alex's voice popped into my head, startling me. *I wish you hadn't said that.*

Of course not. He didn't want me to become immortal, so why would he want me to share anything that could make me seem more than human?

"Interesting." Yelahiah tapped one long silver fingernail against her lips. "That's actually fascinating."

Erin's brows furrowed, but she shook her head. "We can perform a spell and erase her memory. She can leave and won't be tempted to come back. Alex's punishment will be knowing that his soulmate is out there, living her life, and being unable to do a damn thing about it."

"What? No." I clenched my hands. "I refuse to be cursed or hexed, whatever the hell you call it."

"You don't get to make that decision, Matthew," Sterlyn said sternly. "This is a council meeting. When I came here as Griffin's mate, Yelahiah said mates trump the Divine. That applies to Ronnie as well, since she and Alex are not only soulmates, but have completed their bond."

"But she's *human.*" Matthew waved his hand. "She should be turned or sent away. I'm okay with either option."

Azbogah patted Matthew's shoulder. "I must agree with him. Humans aren't meant to be part of this world. Who else votes—"

"No." Yelahiah lifted her hands. "We must consult the doctrine. Yes, she's human, but her mind can't be erased, and she's mated to a vampire. She isn't a normal human, and I'm not sure we have the right to make decisions about someone's humanity in the blink of an eye. I say we move to do more research about any precedents. We can reconvene in a week to discuss this again and vote."

I felt more confident with Yelahiah on our side. I should've known she was a good person since Rosemary was my friend. Most of the time, when someone had such good ethics, they'd learned them from their family members. Or maybe I wanted to believe that because I'd never known my parents.

"Absolutely not." Matthew shook his head. "This is putting my people at risk."

"She can stay with us," Sterlyn offered. "And Alex is welcome too."

"She's a human. We can't let her jeopardize our existence." Azbogah huffed.

"Are you saying your word holds more authority than the Divine?" Pahaliah steepled his fingers. "That was the whole point of creating the Divine—so that one race would not have more say than another. When did that change?"

Azbogah sneered as other members murmured their agreement. He exhaled. "Fine, but she can't leave Shadow City until a plan is in place. And I want to state for the record that allowing a human to stay here puts everything and everyone at risk."

"You've made your stance clear." Griffin slowly rose to his feet. "Since Ronnie is unsafe at the mansion, she should stay with us in our city condo. We don't want her or any of the Shadow City vampires to put their humanity at risk."

Matthew glared at his brother. "Alex still needs to come home with me."

"No," Alex said defiantly. "I am staying with my mate. They've already invited me. I'll be available to you, should you need me."

Breathing deeply, Matthew sneered but said nothing else.

"We'll reconvene in a week." Azbogah stood, determined to be seen as the leader. "Until then, let us reflect deeply on the right course of action for all supernaturals involved."

That was a clear hint on how everyone should vote. A bright neon light saying FORCE HER TO TURN OR LEAVE couldn't have been any more transparent.

"Give me one second," Alex said. He squeezed my hand and rushed to Gwen, leaving me beside Rosemary.

"Are you okay?" Rosemary asked, her eyes more purple than I remembered.

It was the second time within an hour someone had asked me that. I nodded just as Matthew walked up to me, slowing to whisper in my ear, "Don't you find it interesting that he doesn't want you turned? Maybe he doesn't love you after all."

CHAPTER ELEVEN

Alex's adamance that I remain human already bothered me, but Matthew's words echoed my fears, hitting hard. I knew he was trying to undercut my confidence, but the nagging feeling only got worse. "Why are you talking to me?" I tried to deflect and hide that he'd upset me. After all, that was his goal.

"Why would you ask that?" Matthew smiled sweetly, knowing his words had hit as intended. "You are my brother's soulmate."

So, we were going to continue these games.

I'd grown up in a world of fake smiles and insincere words. That was how I'd learned to survive every foster home that had taken me in. If you ticked off your foster parents, they'd send you back. Sometimes that was a blessing and sometimes not, depending on who was managing the group home.

"Why didn't you talk to me about being turned instead of attempting to force my hand?" Yet I'd fallen into the trap of bringing the conversation right back to where he wanted it. But this was the world I was part of now. "He seemed surprised that you were rallying for it."

"The council makes all decisions based on our doctrine—the Divine. Besides, Alex wants you to be here." Matthew waved his hand around the room. "And you've decided to stay. It only makes sense for you to become an official part of it."

In a way, that did sound logical, but I shouldn't be forced into it. It was an irrevocable decision that I couldn't undo if I decided the lifestyle didn't work for me. But to see the pain and torment those vampires had to deal with when they smelled me...I wasn't sure I wanted to live like that either. What if I couldn't control my urges and hurt Annie or Eliza or someone else?

Sterlyn came to my side and grinned at Matthew. "What's going on here?"

"Just having a conversation with the newest member of my family." Matthew placed his hand on my shoulder and leaned into me.

"Isn't that sweet?" She batted her eyes, her sarcasm hitting the mark even harder. "You won't mind sharing what you two were discussing."

"Actually, I do." Matthew stepped in front of me, shielding me from Sterlyn. "You see, I'm her *king*."

"Is that what you think, brother?" Alex sounded playful instead of angry...like he'd caught the tail end of a joke. "She is human, so why would you think that?"

Alex used this tone when he was trying to disarm someone with the intent of proving them wrong.

"She's mated to you." Matthew rubbed his chin. "That means she falls under vampire rule."

"Then she's part of the royal family and deserves a say in vampire affairs, just like Gwen and me." Alex grabbed my hand and pulled me toward him. "Which also allows her a say in whether she turns or not."

Matthew scowled. "She isn't part of the council, so she doesn't get a say."

"What happened to us ruling together and figuring things out as a family?" Alex's tone roughened. "She *is* part of the family, and Gwen and I agree she shouldn't be forced to turn. Why are you going against us?"

"Because you're making me." Matthew clenched a fist. "I told you to stay away from her, but you wouldn't listen. Now you've mated with her. What the *hell* is wrong with you? Is *she* more important than your people?"

"It's funny that you think you know better than fate." Sterlyn stepped around Matthew. She and Alex flanked me, staring down the vampire king together. "If anything, you should let things follow fate's plan instead of forcing your own agenda. We saw how well that worked out for Dick and Saga, didn't we?"

"We said we'd reconvene," Yelahiah said, breaking the tension. "Don't stand here and argue."

My attention flicked to her. Most of the council had been standing there, watching the exchange. Azbogah's eyes seemed darker as he stared at Sterlyn with a scary amount of hate. I didn't know what the hell had happened between them, but there was no love lost there.

Griffin marched toward us, his body coiled, ready to strike. "She's right. Let's take Alex and Veronica to the condo and get them settled in." He regarded the handsome man with the sea-green eyes. "Ezra, is there anything we need to discuss on the shifter front before we leave?"

"Not right this second." Ezra nodded toward the door. "I can run by later to discuss matters."

"Sounds good." Sterlyn placed a hand on my arm. "You are always welcome. I think you know that by now."

Rosemary headed toward her mother. "I'll swing by later."

"Come on," Alex murmured and guided me to the door.

As we exited, he and Sterlyn walked close beside me with Griffin following. They surrounded me in a way that made me feel safe...protected. But I wasn't sure what they were protecting me from. Was it Matthew, the council, or both? For all I knew, it could be for a completely different reason.

Ever since learning about this world, I'd felt like I was in a continuous race to catch up. I'd never imagined living like this, with threats around every corner. I always felt on edge, yet I finally felt at home. Two sides of me warred with each other.

Out in the spacious foyer, I scanned the area for the vampire who'd tried to attack me. He was gone. "Where's the guy who was sweeping?" Terror flitted through me at the thought of him being executed because of me. I didn't want anyone to die because they weren't used to being around humans. That would only prove Matthew's point.

"He's working in the coffee shop's stockroom." Alex tapped his ear. "I can hear him. He's distracted and can't smell you. We're good."

"Okay." Good. It was bad enough that Sergio and the two other workers at the royal home had gotten into trouble. It wasn't their fault they couldn't control themselves around me, although it also wasn't fair for me to be attacked because I had a heartbeat. So many things complicated this situation.

The four of us walked outside, and the beautiful sky stopped me in my tracks. The colors danced around me, and I expected to feel them caress my skin. But the sensation was no different from being outside anywhere else.

"What's wrong?" Alex asked, glancing around.

Sterlyn chuckled. "It's the colors in the air. I remember how stunned I was the first couple of times I saw it. It's gorgeous but disorienting."

That was the perfect description. "I wonder if this is what an acid trip feels like."

"Let's not find out." Alex kissed my cheek. "But, yes, I grew up with it. I was disoriented the first time I stepped out of the city to attend the university two years ago when it opened. You have to remember we weren't allowed to leave the city before then, just like everyone else. We conducted business through the gate with Blade, who managed the Terrace on our behalf."

I hadn't thought of that. Alex had told me they had taken classes inside the city, but when the university opened, he'd started attending to acclimate and learn about modern technology. If he had only been used to this heavenly atmosphere, it would've been strange for him to leave it. And he was much older than I was.

"Did you all drive here?" Since Alex's vehicle was the only car in the parking lot, I assumed they hadn't.

"No, but we'll ride back with you if that's okay." Sterlyn headed toward the Mercedes. "You'll need us to get into the garage."

"Of course." Alex unlocked the vehicle and walked to the passenger door to open it for me.

Not wanting a vampire to stumble across me and attack, I rushed inside. He slammed the door and climbed into the driver's side. Sterlyn sat behind him while Griffin's knees poked my back from behind. I reached down and slid my seat forward to give him more space.

"Sorry, I didn't mean to bump you," Griffin said. "My legs are long."

"I wish I had that problem." I'd always felt short, but nothing compared to being around all these supernaturals. Even the shortest woman had a couple of inches on me.

"Gwen is going to drop off some of our things." Alex turned onto the road, heading away from the mansion. "I hope that's okay. I don't want to take Veronica back there."

"That's fine," Sterlyn said. "We can alert the desk downstairs to let her up when she arrives."

"Are you sure that's smart?" Griffin asked.

Griffin was still hesitant to trust Alex. From what I'd gathered, due to his alpha position and growing up as the son of the alpha of Shadow City, Griffin had received a lot of grief from both the angels and the vampires. Out of everyone, he had the most reason to hold back on trusting them.

"I understand your hesitation." Alex rubbed a hand down his face. "I do. We've given you hell, including me, and I regret many things we've put you through. As far as I'm concerned, you two don't owe me any favors if that improves the situation."

Griffin huffed. "Fine. They can let her up."

More people were out during the day. The streets had been crowded last night, but now they were overflowing with people. It was easier to see how segmented the races were. Angels flew in groups close to the dome. Toned people, who reminded me of Sterlyn and Griffin, stood together, some playing sports in grassy areas. Paler-skinned people, who I assumed were vampires, congregated several feet away from other groups, eyeing them suspiciously. A group surrounding a plant stand had to be witches. When one group passed another, no one waved or made eye contact. They might as well have been invisible to one another.

Alex turned right, onto a side road beside one of the taller buildings glossed in gold. A ginormous sign out front proclaimed it The Elite Wolves' Den in large cursive writing with a wolf print underneath in midnight black. The building was around forty stories high, and when I tried to focus on the top floor, the sun shining through the dome burned my eyes. I blinked away black spots.

"This is it." Griffin leaned forward, pointing to an attached garage. "We park in the lower level."

Alex pulled into the driveway and bore left toward a gate that led downward. He stopped, and I glimpsed back as Sterlyn rolled her window down and pulled a card from her jeans pocket. She scanned the badge, and as soon as the gate rose, Alex coasted through.

Inside the garage, the colorful light disappeared, and I sighed with relief. I was still adjusting to this world.

"Park next to my Navigator," Griffin instructed as we neared the black vehicle in the spot closest to a glass door leading to a glass elevator.

The place reeked of luxury, similar to the vampire mansion. Everyone here must have money, or members of the council did. They were the leaders of the city.

Once we'd pulled into the spot, we all climbed out. My eyes widened at the Porsche and a Viper parked in spots farther from the door.

We took the elevator to the top floor, and I gasped as the view of the city stretched out before my eyes through the floor-to-ceiling glass walls. My stomach dropped to my toes as the elevator rose swiftly into the sky, and within seconds, the doors slid open. We stepped into their home.

Their condo was more modern than the royal mansion, featuring dark platinum-colored tile floors and contrasting stratus-shade walls. The outer walls were all glass, continuing the breathtaking view of the entire city.

The living room looked like something out of a home-decorating catalog with its white leather couches sitting perpendicular to each other and a white coffee table in the center.

A sliding glass door in front of the couches led to a balcony. Substantially as big as the inside, the partially covered balcony had two gold chandeliers hanging over black lounge chairs. One corner housed a bar with a black countertop.

Barely able to believe my eyes, I turned to get my bearings.

"Home sweet home." Sterlyn opened her arms wide. "Please, get comfortable. We'll be spending a lot of time here. I must warn you that Griffin's mom lives here too."

"Oh, okay." Yet another supernatural I'd get to meet. "I really appreciate you letting us stay with you."

Alex placed an arm around my shoulders. "Yes, she wasn't safe at the mansion."

"That's probably why Matthew wants her to turn." Griffin shook his head. "It also figures he'd want to create more vampires."

"Yes, but it won't happen." Alex crossed his arms. "Still, we have to convince at least three others to vote with us."

My throat constricted as his words cut deep. I didn't understand why he was so opposed to me turning. Even if I wasn't sure about it, I wanted him to not despise the thought. We were soulmates. Didn't he want to spend as much time with me as possible?

All the hurt I'd held at bay came crashing over me, flooding me with pain.

Alex glanced at me, his soft blue eyes deepening with concern.

My cell phone rang, startling me. I pulled it from my back pocket and saw Eliza's name flash across the screen.

Shit. Annie had warned me that Eliza might call. For a second, I considered clearing the call, but Eliza deserved better than that. She'd protected me for over five years. "I've got to take this," I explained and walked to a corner of the room for the illusion of privacy.

I steadied myself then answered, "Hello."

"Ronnie Bonds," Eliza said, sounding hurt. "What the hell is going on?"

Okay, she rarely cussed, which meant she was angry...and worried. "I don't know what you mean." Yeah, playing stupid wouldn't work with her.

"Don't you dare be cute," she scoffed. "I expect this behavior from Annie. She's smart and sweet, but not responsible. Not like you. But here you are, throwing your future away for some guy?"

"According to you, I didn't have a future because I spent too much time taking care of you and Annie." That was a regular conversation between us, to the point that I dreaded talking with her at times. "I thought you'd be happy that I figured out where I want to be."

"You know how I feel about that *place*. It's not the same world as here."

"What does that mean?" She kept talking about "that

place" like she knew about Shadow Ridge and Shadow Terrace, but she'd never been here.

"Weird things go on down there." Eliza's voice grew louder. "I told you both that. I want you to come home now."

"No." I'd never defied her before. It hurt to do it, but I couldn't leave Alex. "I'm sorry, but this is where I belong."

She gasped.

Dammit. I didn't mean to hurt her, but I didn't want to string her along either. "Is Annie doing okay?" I wanted to change the subject. I was already hurting, and this conversation was making things worse.

"Yeah, she's fine. I'm so grateful to have her home. But I'm worried about you."

"Take care of her. I'm fine." I pretended to yawn. "I've got to go. I'm tired, but I'll call you later."

"You'd better," she griped, then hung up the phone.

I would need to go back and get my things, but I didn't want to consider what that would do to Eliza. Right now, I had something else I wanted to address. I turned to Alex. *Can we go talk somewhere?* I didn't have time to keep things bottled up. I would get to the bottom of why he was so adamantly against me turning, once and for all.

CHAPTER TWELVE

A lex nodded and eyeballed Sterlyn then Griffin. "Do you mind showing us to our room? I would love to take this blasted jacket off." He rolled his shoulders uncomfortably.

"Sure." Sterlyn removed her black flats and placed them next to the wall. "Do you guys need to borrow any clothes?"

Griffin closed his eyes but kept his mouth shut. He wasn't loving the idea of Alex wearing his clothes.

"I'm fine. Gwen should be here in an hour or so with our things." Alex took my hand and looked at me. "Do you want to change into something? "

"Thanks, but I'm fine too." Hearing that some of our own clothing would be here soon alleviated some stress. Alex taking care of things lessened some of the hurt.

Some.

"Great!" Griffin sighed with relief. "That's for the

best since I'm taller than you and all." He nodded at Alex.

"You don't have to talk him out of it." Sterlyn grinned. "He already said no."

I yawned, not forcing it. Even though I'd fallen asleep in Alex's arms while he'd carried me to his room last night, I hadn't slept well or nearly long enough. So much had happened these past few days that it was hard to comprehend it all.

"I'll take you to your room so you can rest until Gwen gets here." Sterlyn walked to a hallway perpendicular to the living room.

"I'm going to make a few phone calls." Griffin headed for the balcony. "Reception will buzz Gwen in and send her to the guest elevator." He glanced at me. "We came in through the residential entrance. Visitors come up via a guest elevator that leads to an under-cover walkway to the front door so we can control who enters the condo. The front door is that way." He pointed past the residential elevator to another hallway.

"She told me she'll call when she's close." Alex pressed his palm against my back. "I can go down and meet her. I know you're already uncomfortable with my presence here."

The coolness of his hand comforted me. I'd always been partial to heat until lately.

Griffin nodded and went out the sliding glass door.

I turned and followed Sterlyn, realizing she was waiting for us at the end of the hall. I wanted to be alone with Alex. I had so much to say that I was a little overeager to be alone with him.

She lifted a hand toward a closed door on the right. "This is Griffin's and my room. If you need something and we aren't in the living room or kitchen, this is where we'll likely be." She turned left and passed by two more doors across from each other. She gestured to the one on the right, next to their bedroom. "This is our office, but we're rarely in there." She frowned, a bit of sadness bleeding through. "It was where Atticus spent most of his time, and both Griffin and Ulva avoid it."

"Ulva?" I asked. From what I'd gathered from the council meeting, Atticus was Griffin's father.

"Griffin's mom." Sterlyn motioned to the door across from the office. "This is her room."

"That close by?" Alex arched an eyebrow as a naughty smile spread across his face. "Aren't you afraid she'll overhear you and Griffin...you know?"

I smacked his arm in horror. I couldn't believe he'd gone there. "That's none of our business!"

"Your concern is very touching." Sterlyn rolled her eyes. "But she moved out of the master bedroom after Atticus' death. This is the third and final bedroom, and all the rooms are soundproofed."

"Just like home." Alex winked at me. "That's good to know."

My body warmed, betraying me. I wanted to be hurt and mad, not turned on, but I couldn't deny that he cared about me, no matter what Matthew had implied.

"Please wait until you're in your room alone." Sterlyn

waved a hand in front of her nose. "Now I realize why you didn't want to borrow any clothes."

The ground suddenly became very interesting as flames licked my cheeks. I couldn't believe we were having this discussion.

"Aw, you're embarrassed, Veronica." Alex kissed my forehead, making the situation worse.

"Yeah, that was me a few months ago." Sterlyn chuckled and walked to the last door on the right. "And this is the master bedroom, which you can use."

Alex sniffed. "We're staying in Ulva and Atticus's old room."

Sterlyn opened the door and moved out of the way. "Yes. You two get some rest. It's been a long night. After this morning, everyone is on edge. A nap will do you good."

I hadn't considered that Alex might not have slept well last night, proving I was being a little self-absorbed.

I entered the room and took in our surroundings. The room was half the size of Alex's back at the mansion but at least three times the size of my bedroom in Lexington. A king-sized bed abutted the center of the left wall. White netting cascaded from its black canopy and was tied to a post at each corner of the bed. Wrinkle-free, coffee-toned bedding warmed the décor, appearing soft and inviting. The wall to the right of the bed offered a floor-to-ceiling view of the city.

"Let us know if you need anything." Sterlyn focused on me before shutting the door.

Nerves took over, so I strolled to the window overlooking the city. The shifting colors danced in the sky, blending and weaving into one another. Unlike the uniform architecture in both Shadow Terrace and Shadow Ridge, the buildings here were quite varied. The taller buildings were made of golden metal, while the smaller buildings were brick or resembled a white Grecian style of architecture.

"Are you okay?" Alex asked. "I overheard your conversation with Eliza."

"It's fine. I want to talk with you about earlier, not Eliza."

"I didn't mean to be an ass." Alex came over and stood beside me, following my gaze. "I was rude. But you've seemed off since the council meeting. I wanted to make you smile, but I don't feel like myself either, and I wound up acting kind of weird."

"Kind of?" I'd meant to tease him, but the words came out critical instead. I couldn't hide the hurt now that it was just the two of us.

"Yes, I was being a...what do you call it? Dude?" His brows furrowed.

I laughed despite myself. "I think you mean douche."

He shrugged off his black suit jacket and tossed it onto the bed. "What's wrong?"

That was a loaded question. I didn't want to seem insecure, but everything I wanted to start with would make me sound that way.

"Look, I don't want you to worry." He took my hand and turned me toward him. "I won't allow them to turn you."

And there it was.

The problem.

"Even if it means going back to Eliza's with my memory erased?" The witches seemed certain that their spell would work.

"If that's what it takes." He lowered his forehead to mine.

Before our heads touched, I moved back. "So, this whole 'soulmates' thing isn't as big of a deal as you made it out to be."

Wariness etched into his face. "I'm not sure what you're saying."

"You would rather not have me in your life than have me turned." My voice rose slightly, making me sound weak. "This whole connection is forgettable to you."

"Wait." He ran his fingers through his hair, mussing it. "Do you *want* to be turned?"

"I don't know." That was the truth, and he'd know if I was lying.

"Then why are you upset?" He dropped his hands to his sides. "You aren't sure what you want. I'm trying to make sure you have time to think everything through and not feel pressured into anything."

"But—" I stopped, realizing that dancing around this was futile. I had to say how I felt, or resentment would fester inside me. "You should want me to turn. I thought you wanted to be with me forever."

"Wow," he said in surprise, taking a step back and twirling a finger in front of him. "Let me make sure I understand. You aren't sure if you want to be turned, and you're upset because I don't want to force you to turn?"

Okay, now *he* was making me sound unreasonable. "Not force. But...why wouldn't you want me to be turned? Is there something wrong with me?"

"No. Absolutely not." He rubbed his hands together. "That's why I don't want you to turn."

"Because you wouldn't find me desirable if I were a vampire?"

"Of course, I would. I'd find you sexy no matter what." He gritted his teeth. "It has nothing to do with finding you attractive or wanting to be with you."

"Yes, it does!" My voice rose again, and I winced. Thank God this room was soundproof. "You don't want me to turn. You'd rather I go back to my human life and not remember you. How does that prove you want to be with me?"

"How does it not?" Alex took hold of my hands and held them to his chest. "Your life and happiness mean so much more to me than mine. I'd rather you forget me and find someone else who would love you as I stood by, heartbroken, to protect your soul from being damned. I'll sacrifice everything to protect you."

I inhaled sharply, taking in the magnitude of what he'd dropped on me. "What do you mean, *damned*?"

"When a vampire submits to their cravings and loses control—which gets easier to do each time—they're damned to the fiery pits of Hell." He squeezed my hands gently. "And it's hard to ignore those cravings at times— especially for someone who is newly turned. I could never forgive myself if I was selfish enough to turn you, and then you gave in to your newborn cravings, and your humanity slipped away."

God, I'd been so stupid. Here I'd thought he didn't want to be with me forever, and his only concern was making sure I didn't turn into the very creature he fought every day.

Standing on my tiptoes, I kissed him. I pulled back and sighed. "I'm sorry. It's just that when you were so adamantly against me being turned, I was afraid you thought our being together would be more permanent than you'd thought, and you might not want that. We hadn't talked about it. Hell, you didn't even tell me that turning was a possibility."

"An eternity with you wouldn't be long enough." He brushed my cheek with his fingertips and said, "I want you by my side forever, but I don't want to influence you with my selfish desire. You can't undo becoming a vampire."

Needing to be closer to him, I pressed my body to his. Warmth flared through me, and I wanted to show him how much I loved him, too. "I can't forget you. I won't. I'm the happiest I've ever been because of you."

I needed him. My body ached for him. Frantic, I unfastened and unzipped his slacks, my intention very clear.

"You have time to decide, and if you decide you don't want to turn, we will find a way out of this." He groaned as I stroked him. "I'd rather pay attention to this moment and you."

The power I had over him exhilarated me. I smiled then kissed him again, backing him up to the bed. "I can get behind that."

His fingers dug into my hips. "I guess you better turn around."

We blurred, and before I knew what was happening, my upper thighs and knees hit the mattress. He yanked my skirt up and my panties down. "Step out of them," he commanded.

If I hadn't been turned on before, I damn sure was now. We'd never had sex like this, and it felt invigorating. We were desperate for each other.

I moaned as I glanced back. *Kiss me, dammit.* If he could be bossy, so could I.

A deep, sexy-as-hell chuckle came from him. He dropped his pants and boxers and stepped toward me. His lips pressed to mine, and he slipped his tongue into my mouth as he positioned himself behind me. I spread my legs and leaned over, about to plead for him to enter me.

He thrust inside me, slipping one hand down my shirt and into my bra to flick my nipple as his free arm wrapped around me. The palm of his hand settled on my pelvis, and his fingers slipped between my legs, placing pressure on me and keeping me in place as he stroked me to ecstasy.

The friction built, and he slammed inside me harder and harder. Unable to hold myself in position to kiss him any longer, I laid my head on the mattress as his body and hands worked magic over me in ways I'd never felt before.

His sweet smell surrounded me, and as he catered to my every need, I felt safe and loved.

I love you, I gasped through our bond.

You are my everything, he connected and pushed his love toward me.

I couldn't believe I'd ever doubted it. I hated that I'd questioned his commitment to me.

His body quivered, and I fell over the edge with him. Our orgasms collided, the intensity overwhelming.

As we caught our breath, I flipped over to face him. He wrapped his arms around my body and pulled me close. We lay there, half naked, holding on to each other, clinging to the moment.

His phone dinged from somewhere on the floor, and he moaned as he released his hold. "I bet it's Gwen."

"Go check." I brushed my lips over his. "If it's her, we don't need to aggravate Griffin any more than we already have."

"You're right." He bent down, picked up his slacks, and pulled out his phone, frowning as annoyance flowed between us.

"What's wrong?" I bet it wasn't Gwen.

He laughed without humor. "Oh, Matthew is here and wants to talk." He locked eyes with me as he scowled. "Alone."

"Oh, hell no." The prick was rallying people to force me into a decision to turn. He didn't get to make any more demands. "I'm going with you."

CHAPTER THIRTEEN

Mustering as much dignity as I could, I stood and pulled my panties up and my skirt down. I hadn't even taken my shoes off.

"You know what?" Alex dressed himself and leaned over to kiss my cheek. "You're right. We're a package deal. He needs to accept that."

I'd expected him to tell me to stay put, so for him to side with me meant more to me than he'd ever know. I ran my fingers through my copper hair to tame it.

"But if anything happens with him, I want you to come back inside." He stared into my eyes. "Promise me."

That was fair. I didn't want to deal with any of Matthew's tricks. "Of course. I don't want you to get hurt either." And he would try to protect me.

He held my hand and tugged me to the door. "Come on. I don't want him to come up here and upset Griffin."

If I hadn't seen Griffin's reaction to Gwen and Matthew, I'd have thought he still hated Alex. But after seeing him glare at them, I could discern a marked difference in his attitude toward my soulmate.

We were walking toward the living room when an unfamiliar voice drifted down the hall.

"We have a vampire and his mate staying here," the woman said with surprise. "Those are words I never expected to hear in my lifetime." She chuckled warmly, easing some of my worry.

Alex laughed as we entered the room. Griffin, Sterlyn, and a woman in a navy sundress stood in the center. The woman appeared to be in her forties with striking, sapphire-blue eyes and golden-blond hair that brushed her shoulders.

The lady smiled. "And these must be the guests of honor."

I hated being the center of attention. "I'm not so sure about honor. I think we're more guests due to my being human."

"Don't mind Ronnie." Sterlyn walked around the couch and placed an arm around my shoulders. "She has a way of acting like she's an inconvenience, even though we don't remotely feel that way."

"That's true." Griffin smirked. "But don't get her too confident. I like her thinking she's indebted to us."

Alex tensed.

"He's kidding." The older woman glared at Griffin. "Apologize."

That expression resembled the one Griffin used when he was annoyed. This had to be his mother.

"They know I was kidding." Griffin's shoulders

sagged. "If you haven't guessed, this is my mom, Ulva. And Mom, this is Ronnie." He placed his hands in his pockets.

Sterlyn dropped her arm. "I'm sure she figured that out."

"I hate to be rude and interrupt," Alex started just as a loud knock sounded at the door. He mashed his lips into a line. "But Matthew is here."

A low growl emanated from Griffin's chest. "I thought you said you were meeting Gwen outside. Dammit, I didn't specify that the visitor was a woman, so the front desk let that prick up the guest elevator."

"That was the plan." Alex rocked on his heels. "But Matthew took our things from Gwen and headed over. I was hoping we could head him off outside."

"You were going outside with Ronnie?" Sterlyn's irises deepened to an orchid. "What if there are vampires outside?"

Nope, he wouldn't catch hell on this decision. "I want to be there. How will Matthew take me seriously if I don't stand by Alex's side?"

"Look, I get that." Sterlyn placed her hands on her hips. "Seriously. I was in the same situation with Griffin, not that long ago. Hell, I kind of still am. Things have been on hold because Dick is gone, but whether it's right or wrong, you're human. There *is* an added risk for you that there wasn't for me."

"In other words, I don't belong here." I couldn't hide the pain her words had caused. I'd banked on her having my back. Despite her concern coming from a place of love, it still hurt to hear her lay it all out there.

"What? No!" Sterlyn stole my hand from Alex's and held it firmly. "You belong here. I feel it. I knew it that first night I met you, but this world is more dangerous for you."

Matthew pounded harder on the door.

That man could add patience to his ever-growing list of missing attributes.

Ulva rolled her eyes. "I'll go let the impatient blood-sucker in." She winced and placed her hands together, turning her attention to Alex. "No offense."

"None taken." Alex laughed. "But I can talk to him outside."

"No," Sterlyn said. "We have to let him in. If we confirm we don't want him in here, he'll stir up more trouble with the council. I bet he's hoping we don't allow him inside, and that's why he didn't wait to be invited up."

"You're right." Alex's frown was set so deep that I finally understood the cliché phrase *turn that frown upside down*. "Why do I keep letting him get the upper hand?"

"Because he's your brother." Ulva strolled past the elevator, down the hallway, and to the front door. "We always want to see the good in our family."

The simple truth of her words sank in. She was right. I'd only wanted to see the good in Annie, even when her mind had been messed with. I never saw the crazy, just the sweet, loving girl I'd always known was inside her.

"Did Killian ever make it back okay?" I felt like an ass since I hadn't even thought about him. He was the one making a ten-hour drive on no sleep.

"Yeah, Killian's heading home now." Griffin tapped his head. "He linked with us while you were in the room..." He trailed off and pulled at his collar.

Wait... Panic clawed inside me. *Does he know we had sex?*

We smell like sex. Alex grinned, not ashamed at all. *It's fine. We're soulmates.*

Great, that meant Matthew would be able to tell as well. Privacy didn't exist in this world. But I needed to focus before Matthew came in here and derailed the conversation. "Why is Killian just getting home? I figured he'd have been back early this morning."

"He stayed and watched Annie to make sure her memory was adequately erased and nothing strange happened, like a vampire following them." Sterlyn sat on the couch that faced the hallway to the front door. "He reached out to a local pack there, and they'll keep an eye on your family for the next few days for security."

I hadn't considered that Annie and Eliza could be in danger. This close group of friends kept protecting me and those I loved. It was a good thing they didn't keep track of favors because it'd take a lifetime, if not longer, to repay them. "Thank you."

We should sit, Alex connected with me and touched my arm, indicating I should follow him. *We don't want Matthew to see us on edge.*

That had to be why Sterlyn had sat down, but

frankly, we were on edge, especially poor Griffin, who kept opening up his home to vampires when he didn't want to. If not for Sterlyn, we wouldn't have made it very far with him.

We sat on the couch across from her, our backs to the elevator. It didn't sit well with me that our backs would be toward Matthew when he entered, but Sterlyn had taken the couch with the best vantage point, and it would be plain weird for all four of us to be squashed on it together.

Griffin blew a raspberry and sat next to Sterlyn. She placed her hand on his leg just as I heard Ulva's footsteps heading back into the room.

"I think this is the first time you've ever visited us here," Ulva said kindly as she and Matthew joined us.

I looked over my shoulder.

Matthew had changed into khakis and a fitted shirt that made him appear scrawny compared to Griffin and Alex. A black bag hung off his shoulder, emphasizing that he was nowhere near as muscular as Griffin. He had a slender frame rather than an athletic build, like Alex. He was handsome because, hell, all supernaturals were, but he paled in comparison to Alex. No pun intended.

The vampire king's jaw twitched, and he hissed at Alex, "I thought you'd come outside so we could talk alone."

"Veronica and I were on our way out to meet you, but you got impatient—" Alex started.

"Again, I want to talk to you *alone*." Matthew's shoulders tensed, causing the black bag to swing, and he gestured to the balcony. "Let's go out there."

"And vampires say that wolves are animals." Griffin crossed his arms. "Yet he comes in here without saying hello or being polite to my mother, then makes demands."

"Honey." Sterlyn laid her head on his shoulder, her body anything but relaxed. "What do you expect from someone who backstabbed his brother? He knows niceties won't get him far."

Yeah, I was enjoying this way too much. I should have been upset that Alex and his brother were at odds, but Matthew was the problem. He kept pushing Alex away. I wasn't putting Alex in that position. Granted, I wished it hadn't come to this.

"You do realize I'm a council member too, and the king of the vampires." Matthew stood as still as a statue. Only his moving lips proved he was alive.

"How could we forget, dear brother?" Alex twisted toward him, his back against my shoulder. "You remind everyone as often as possible."

"Don't you dare act better than me." Matthew pointed his finger as if it were a weapon. "Not even three weeks ago, you were by my side, backing my decisions. Now you've let a girl come in and mess with everything!"

Ulva stood there wearing an unreadable expression.

"Thank God she did." Griffin motioned to me. "Because you and Alex were incorrigible and had no one's interests at heart but your own."

"Do not talk down to me." Matthew marched into the

living room and stood in front of the couches. "I deserve respect."

"Respect is earned, not given." Yeah, I should have let them hash this out, but I hated people who thought that just because they were born into money, power, or whatever, they were entitled to respect. "You were born with the duty of working for the crown bestowed upon you. From what I can see, you haven't done a damn thing to earn it."

Sterlyn smiled at me. "Perfectly said."

Matthew sneered. "Fine, it's best if I tell all of you this at the same time anyway." He tossed the bag at my feet. "There was a concern that you might sneak Veronica out of Shadow City to prevent her from being turned if we decided on that fate."

"Why would we do that?" Alex breathed heavily. He couldn't lose his composure. That had to be why Matthew had wanted to tell him alone—to antagonize his brother.

I looped my arm through his, hoping my touch would calm him. Luckily, it worked a little.

"Well," Matthew said with a laugh, "because obviously, you don't think clearly when it comes to her. You might run off with her, which would cause problems, not only for me but for the entire council. Each leader needs to have a strong hold over their people." He smirked.

Even if I'd wanted to run, I wouldn't.

Sterlyn lifted her chin. "I'm assuming a plan was concocted to ease the worry."

"That is one thing I admire about you, silver wolf."

Matthew glared at her despite his praise. "You are smart and have a head for strategy."

"Yet it doesn't feel like you complimented me." She arched a brow.

"He's worried the silver wolves will make a comeback and take over protecting both sides of the river," Alex tossed out there. "Isn't that right, brother?"

The smugness fell from Matthew's face like he'd been slapped.

"If you're concerned about that, maybe there's a reason," Griffin said as he intertwined his fingers with Sterlyn's.

Ulva intervened, redirecting the conversation. "I'm guessing there's more news about what the council wishes to do about Veronica, then." Her poise was similar to Sterlyn's, indicating she also knew how to lead.

"There will be a daily check-in from someone on the council outside of this group." Matthew's gloating demeanor fell back into place. "Don't get any ideas about taking matters into your own hands."

"Don't worry," Alex said through gritted teeth. "We won't."

"Good." He nodded at the bag. "Your belongings are in there, and I won't need you this week. Enjoy the time you have together." He spun on his heels and marched to the front door without saying goodbye.

If that wasn't a threat, I didn't know what was.

The five of us glanced back and forth between ourselves as the door slammed.

"That could've gone better." Ulva sighed as she strolled over and sat next to Sterlyn.

"I'm not sure it could've." Alex's head lowered, and hurt wafted through our bond. "He's angry and lashing out. He's unpredictable when he gets like that."

"What do you mean?" I nibbled on my bottom lip. "Do you think he'll try something?"

Alex huffed. "Oh, yeah. He will."

Sterlyn leaned back into the seat and stared outside at the balcony. "What do you think he'll do?"

"I have no clue." Alex pulled me into his arms. "But we'll find out soon."

THE NEXT FEW days went by without incident. I talked with Eliza daily and exchanged several text messages with Annie. Things were tense, and Annie seemed distant. I wasn't sure how to help either of them since I was locked in Shadow City.

One thing I'd learned was that Alex and Griffin were truly competitive with each other. They played chess every night while Sterlyn, Ulva, and I sat on the balcony, drinking wine. We could hear them threatening each other in low hisses and growls, which somehow bonded them—something I would've never guessed could happen, but Ulva assured me it was an alpha male tendency, and everything was okay.

Sterlyn shared stories about her parents and former pack life. Her twin brother, Cyrus, was her beta, and he was taking on alpha duties while she and Griffin focused on straightening things out with the council. He checked in with her nightly as the silver wolves finished settling into a nearby pack neighborhood about twenty minutes away from Shadow Ridge.

Killian also checked in regularly. He was keeping a tight guard over Shadow Ridge, making sure the rogue vampires didn't enter the city, while Sierra tried to find out anything she could at the bar where she worked. Nothing substantial had come up, but they were keeping an eye on things.

All was going amazingly well, other than me being trapped inside the condominium. Yelahiah, Gwen, then Pahaliah had made the first few check-ins. Today was the first day that someone who wasn't in my corner would be visiting.

I hated that Griffin's childhood home had become a revolving door for the council, but we couldn't do much about it at the moment.

Alex paced in front of the couch I was sitting on as we waited for Azbogah to arrive.

"He's only five minutes late," I tried to reassure Alex. "And Griffin is bringing him here after a meeting. If there was a problem, he'd have let Sterlyn know by now."

"Azbogah's never late." Alex grunted. "He thinks being on time is late."

That sounded like the dark angel.

I stood and hugged him. "Hey, it's going to be okay. Maybe he's trying to make us sweat."

Sterlyn rushed into the living room, her skin nearly the same color as her silver hair.

"What's wrong?" Alex asked, on the brink of a meltdown.

"There's an attack happening at the council building," she rasped and grabbed the Navigator keys from the counter.

CHAPTER FOURTEEN

I must have misunderstood her—but the way she raced to the elevator proved I hadn't.

"Dammit," Alex hissed as he pulled me after her.

"No." Sterlyn shook her head, the keys dangling in her hand. "You two stay here."

"Look, I'm not pleased about it, but if Matthew is involved in the attack, I need to be there, and Ronnie needs to go with us too." His hand tightened around mine. "We can't leave her alone. For all we know, an angel could land on the balcony and force their way in."

However, my presence might make the situation worse. "I think it'll be okay. Why don't you two go, and I'll stay here?"

"Not an option." Alex pulled me close to his side. "Don't get me wrong, I'd rather you stay here, but you could be in danger."

"Alex is right. The attack could be a diversion."

Sterlyn bounced on her toes. "You should come with us. And why the hell is the elevator taking so long?"

"Are there stairs for emergencies?" I glanced around the room as if they would magically appear. I hadn't left the condo in days, so I knew there weren't.

The doors slid open, and Sterlyn raced inside. "There are, but the location is a secret and leads to a hidden way out of the building. Besides, the elevator will take less time."

Good to know. Maybe.

We descended in silence, though Sterlyn fidgeted constantly. Her irises were a dark purple, conveying how worried she was about Griffin.

Alex wasn't much better, though he wasn't quite as on edge. In fairness, her mate was in danger.

In the garage, Sterlyn ran to the Navigator, and Alex stopped, forcing me to stay beside him.

Before I could question him, Sterlyn jumped into the vehicle and peeled out of the parking spot. She slammed on the brakes, which made the tires squeal and burn rubber.

I'd never seen her this worried, and her reaction had me panicking. She was usually the calm one of the group. I hadn't realized how much I depended on her levelheadedness. A bit of hysteria bubbled inside me.

Alex opened the door, picked me up, then climbed inside the car. He shut the door and nestled me on his lap as Sterlyn jetted off. "Why are we driving? I thought you all walked around here?"

"My wolf can sustain high speeds only for short

distances, so the car is faster. Besides, we can't run with you in tow." She flew up the ramp, and the gate had barely risen out of the way before she blew through and turned sharply onto the main road.

The Navigator tipped onto the two wheels on the driver's side, but Sterlyn didn't let up on the gas.

"Sterlyn, slow down," Alex groaned as he threw his weight to the passenger side, and the vehicle landed back on four wheels, jarring us.

My head snapped and a sickening crack sounded at the base of my neck. A sharp pain flared down my spine, and I rolled my head around to relieve it. Luckily, I could still move, and the sharpness dulled.

"I can't," Sterlyn said. Her hands clutched the wheel, and her attention stayed focused on the road. She blew her horn, and my attention flicked outside.

Unlike the last time we'd driven through the city, people were rushing off the roads and backing away from the sidewalks and against the buildings as the vehicle barreled down the street. The calm, easygoing feel of the city had transformed into panic as Sterlyn sped toward the council building.

If we got there in one piece, it would be a miracle.

"Have you considered that whoever is attacking hopes you won't be thinking clearly?" Alex growled, visibly unhappy. "You could be playing right into their hands."

"Ugh, you're right." She exhaled and slowed down. "It's just...if something were to happen to Griffin—" She stopped, unable to finish the thought.

She didn't have to, though. Alex and I understood all too well. Just the thought of not having him by my side sent a burning sensation through my chest like my heart was being ripped from my body. I could only imagine how it would feel if I were at risk of losing Alex like she was going through with Griffin.

"You can still feel him, right?" Alex asked carefully.

"Yes." She ran a hand through her hair and yanked it behind her shoulder. "That's why I slowed down. If the connection had vanished or gone cold, I'd be driving way faster."

Hell, if I were in her position, even knowing Alex was okay wouldn't put me at ease. I'd be desperate to reach him.

The residents on the sidewalks were back to normal. Everyone was meandering around and chatting, except for a group of people standing on a corner two blocks away from the council building. Fifteen figures with sour expressions on their faces split their attention between the council building and themselves.

One gestured at us; her poppy-red hair was brighter than my own, and her short stature made her stand out from the crowd. Her eyes were so bright that even I could make out the sparkling emerald irises, which contrasted with her faint golden complexion. She closed her eyes and pinched the bridge of her nose.

She looked guilty of something.

We drove by, and I gasped as the front of the council building came into view. Twenty people dressed in black from head to toe milled in front of the entrance, their faces covered in ski masks and their hands in gloves.

"Holy shit." Sterlyn pulled into the parking lot. "They're dressed like the people who slaughtered my pack."

My stomach turned. What kind of world had I gotten mixed up with?

The assailants were pummeling Azbogah, Griffin, and Matthew with poles. The three council members had formed a circle, their backs to one another as the horde descended on them.

Alex's trepidation wafted through to me as he watched his brother in danger.

Sterlyn parked and jumped out of the car to run to her mate, not bothering to shut the door. She ran to the tallest person in black and kneed them in the crotch.

The figure groaned loudly as they fell to the ground, cupping their groin.

Sterlyn rushed to the next attacker and elbowed them in the neck. She worked efficiently and with a brute strength that awed me.

Alex could help them, but he didn't want to leave me. I wanted to help Griffin after everything he'd done for me, but I was learning that, in this world, I was more of a liability than an asset. "We can't sit here and do nothing." I had to put Alex's needs above mine. If he didn't help and something happened to Matthew, he would blame himself.

"Ugh, fine." Alex sighed and opened the door. He climbed out and turned to me. "Stay here and lock the doors. If anyone makes a move toward you, holler, and I'll be back in a flash."

"Just go." I hated that he was putting himself at risk, but I'd held him back too much, especially where his family was concerned. "I'll be fine."

He nodded and quickly kissed me, then ran around the car and slammed Sterlyn's door closed before racing into the melee. I locked the doors and leaned forward between the seats, over the center console, to watch the fight. If things got worse, I'd be joining them.

I watched Alex work side by side with Sterlyn. The two of them weaved back and forth, taking out individuals on the outer edges.

A masked figure swung their pole and smacked Griffin in the head. Griffin's face turned red, and he picked up the person and launched them over the entire group. The figure flew through the air and landed on their back.

Not only was Sterlyn a force of nature, but so was her mate. Seeing them fight together made me realize why Matthew feared them. Not only that, but their relationship was based on mutual respect, not dominance, a rare quality in the supernatural hierarchy.

My attention flicked to Matthew. His three attackers barely swung their poles at him and came nowhere close to actually hitting the vampire king.

That was odd.

I glanced at Azbogah, who had four attackers on him, but just like Matthew, they weren't trying to hurt him.

They did enough to give the impression that they were attacking him.

This was a setup.

Jumping out of the vehicle, I raced to Sterlyn and Alex. "Focus on helping Griffin."

Sterlyn pivoted toward me, asking, "What do you mean?"

"Abort," a masked man shouted. "Get out of here."

Chaos ensued as people ran in different directions, and Sterlyn raced to her mate. Griffin had cuts on his face, and blood trickled down the sides.

Azbogah and Matthew didn't have a scratch on them.

The guy Sterlyn had kicked in the nuts was lying at my feet and got up. He took a hurried step to run away, and I pivoted, moving faster than ever before, and nailed him between his legs again. He fell to the ground again with a thud.

"You aren't getting away," I promised and leaned over him.

A strangled roar escaped him, and his eyes took on a catlike quality. Whoa, he had to be a cat shifter. Terror coiled inside me. This was my future—one fight after another—and it had taken this attack for that to fully sink in.

All the races were in conflict with one another, and they all wanted to eliminate whatever threat they perceived, even if it wasn't legitimate.

If I became a vampire, would I become like the rest of them? Would it put Sterlyn and me at odds? Growing old in front of Alex would hurt, but so would losing the friendships I'd forged. Each person completed me in a way I needed, and I didn't want to lose any of them. But to live in their world, I'd have to deal with constant threats and turmoil.

Alex flashed beside me and kicked the guy in the head, knocking him out cold. He turned and scanned me for injuries. *Are you okay? I told you to stay put.*

I didn't want all of them to get away. I ignored his question and focused on his statement. If I tried to tell him how I was, I'd freak out, and I refused to do that in front of Matthew and Azbogah.

The way the attackers had scattered so easily validated what I'd seen from the car. Griffin had taken the brunt of the attack. *Alex, I'm not trying to make things worse.* I needed to use my heightened emotions to my advantage while I could. *But I got out of the car because Matthew and Azbogah weren't truly being attacked.*

What? Alex asked, following my gaze.

They aren't injured, and they didn't stop anyone from running off. I hated to speak ill of his brother, but Alex had guessed he was up to something. *I think your brother might have planned this, but I don't know why.*

Alex turned his back to his brother, and his expression crumpled into heartbreak. *I do.*

His sense of betrayal slammed into me, and I wrapped my arm around his waist, trying to be there for him. *I don't follow.*

The attackers were shifters. Alex's hands clenched into fists.

They'd been covered from head to toe. *How do you know that?*

He tapped his nose. *They had a musky smell. Various scents, but all shifter races have an animalistic musk.*

"Thank God you caught one," Sterlyn said from behind us. "I was so focused on Griffin that the thought didn't cross my mind."

I spun around to see her and Griffin standing over the unconscious man.

Matthew's lips pressed tight, and his eyes cut to Azbogah.

Yeah, something fishy was going on between them. But why would they have coordinated this?

Questions swirled inside my head as Azbogah's ebony eyes focused on me with so much hatred that his vileness washed over me.

The shadow appeared beside him.

I swayed as the turmoil from the last month swirled inside until I couldn't breathe. I was choking, drowning in worry and confusion.

This was my breaking point.

My chest shook. No matter how hard I tried to fill my lungs, they wouldn't expand.

"Veronica!" Alex exclaimed, his arms wrapping around my body.

His panic combined with mine, intensifying the feeling. I fell to my knees as the colorful lights in the air danced around me, mocking me.

I hadn't had a panic attack in years. The best thing I

could do was calm down, but I couldn't focus on anything.

Continuous danger, turmoil, and backstabbing were constant. Everywhere I turned, someone had ulterior motives. These people didn't value any life besides their own.

The simplest thing to do would be to leave, but that wasn't an option. No matter where I went, someone would hunt me down. I felt it in my bones.

I hadn't fully understood how much peril I was in until now. My head grew dizzy, and I heard Alex yell, "You've got to help her."

A moment later, something cracked against my cheek, causing blinding pain.

CHAPTER FIFTEEN

"Ouch," I whined and rubbed my cheek, but the weight on my chest eased. "That hurt."

Alex glared at Sterlyn; his fangs descended as his vampire side bled through.

Sterlyn ignored him, still leaning over me with her hair hanging around her face. Her sweet, musky, floral scent and calm demeanor, now back in place, eased some of my panic. She looked normal, like the woman I'd known for almost a month.

She scanned me over. "I'm sorry, but you were spiraling. I wasn't sure what else to do."

"You didn't have to hit her that hard," Alex hissed, his words nearly indistinguishable. "You're a silver wolf, for crying out loud."

"It's fine." She had hit me hard, but I had a feeling she'd held back. I moved my jaw from side to side to work out the dull ache.

"You hit a member of the royal vampire family,"

Matthew said with disgust, rushing past the unconscious shifter to my side as if he cared. "You cannot do that. There are consequences for such actions."

Now he wanted to feign concern when it worked in his favor. "She did it to help me. No punishment needed." I stood and walked to Alex's other side, refusing to remain beside the traitor.

Alex brushed his fingertips across my cheek, and I winced. "I get that it snapped you out of your state, but we could've tried softer ways first."

I captured his hand in mine as a chill ran down my spine. "Believe me, snapping me out of that quickly was the softest way." Remembering what had caused me to spiral, I turned to Azbogah.

Thankfully, the shadow was gone, but Azbogah's nose wrinkled with disgust.

Had I imagined the shadow?

"The girl isn't suited for this world," Azbogah said. "And Sterlyn and Griffin are losing control over the shifters."

"That's not true," Griffin growled, squatting next to the man dressed in black. "Nothing like this has happened before."

"Really?" Azbogah arched an eyebrow. "Nothing? What about all those shifter attacks not even three months ago? Several of them targeted your mate."

I wanted to yell *setup*, but I kept my mouth shut. To outwit egotistical asshole men, you couldn't come at them head on, not at first. It was best to make their story crumble around them, then kick them between the legs.

"Dick and Saga were behind those attacks. I sincerely doubt they planned this one." Glowering, Griffin grabbed the bottom of the guy's mask and pulled it off his face. "Dammit, this is one of the panthers."

The man had thin, luminous black hair and scruff that complemented his dark olive skin. His face was sharp and angular, reminding me of a cat. He was stunning, even though, in my eyes, he didn't hold a candle to Alex.

Matthew straightened and waved a finger around. "You put Dick in charge."

"Are we going to stand around and continue this pissing match?" Sterlyn gestured to the unconscious man. "Because Griffin's and my time could be put to better use by questioning the guy to learn why they attacked."

"So, you don't know." Azbogah *tsk*ed. "That doesn't bode well for the shifter representatives on the council."

"I'm sure you know everything going on with the angels." Sterlyn arched an eyebrow in a dare.

He laughed loudly. "Of course, I do. I have eyes and ears everywhere. It's part of being an amazing leader."

"Or a tyrant." Alex turned so I was mostly behind him. "Isn't that right, dear brother?"

If someone didn't get a handle on the situation, things would get worse, and fast. "Everyone has a right to freedom as long as they follow the law." Wasn't that the dream? To do what you wanted so long as you did no harm to yourself or others?

"This is why I'm petitioning for her to turn." Matthew frowned and leered at me as if I were a mere annoyance. "That is how humans live, not supernaturals."

"Who's to say that isn't what we're trying to achieve?" Sterlyn countered, her irises glowing. "You don't get to decide for all races."

"No, he doesn't." Azbogah nodded, then fluffed his feathers behind his back. "But I agree with his sentiment, as do many others. We don't have time for foolish ideals or human fragility."

Yeah, these two jackasses were working together. Before, I'd been guessing, but this act of superiority confirmed it. "Aren't shifters part human, and don't most vampires retain their humanity? How is that a bad thing?"

"Let's see." Azbogah pivoted around Alex and strolled over to me, forcing me to tilt my head back to look into his eyes.

He wanted to intimidate me, but I refused to cower. I straightened my shoulders the best I could and stepped around Alex to stand on my own.

Honeysuckle hit my nose, reminding me of Rosemary's floral scent. I wondered if that was a common attribute of angels, similar to the sweet smells of vampires and musk of shifters.

"We have two shifter council members here who may agree with that sentiment, yet one of their own representatives was just viciously attacked, along with me and Matthew." The dark angel extended his wings behind him, casting a shadow over me. "And we have a vampire with his humanity who brought his mate into a supernatural world where the majority of the city residents have never been exposed to a human before."

Something inside me ran cold, and the urge to step out of Azbogah's shadow overwhelmed me.

He ruffled his feathers, and Alex intervened.

Alex's teeth were back to normal, but red still bled into his eyes. "We opened the city gates to allow a select few to assimilate, like the students approved to attend Shadow Ridge University, along with Gwen, Matthew, and me to help govern Shadow Terrace as intended. Those are the same reasons Griffin and Sterlyn can leave. It's better for a vampire with their humanity intact to have a human mate, because they can keep them grounded and help them avoid temptation. Believe me, I'd know."

"That's enough," Matthew warned, tugging at the collar of his canary-yellow shirt. "We don't need to be enemies. We need the wolves to explain what the hell is going on."

"To do that, we need to question the panther." Griffin grabbed the man's arm and dragged him toward the Navigator.

The guy resembled a panther now that I was examining him.

"Where are you taking him?" Matthew asked anxiously.

Sterlyn took hold of the man's ankles and lifted the panther off the ground. She made carrying him look easy, more so than Griffin. She nodded toward the Navigator. "To Shadow City Jail for questioning. Where else?"

"Let me help," Matthew volunteered, which seemed uncharacteristic for him. "I know you need to take Veronica back to the condo before someone attacks her."

"I suspect you'd enjoy that." The words fell from my mouth, and I wasn't even apologetic about it. "It would help enforce your stance."

Alex chuckled and placed an arm around my shoulders. "She's right. The night we arrived here, why didn't you warn Sergio so he wouldn't attack her? If anyone is losing control over their people, it's us."

"Is she worth it?" Matthew rasped, his nostrils flaring. "You're letting a *human* come between us and our people."

"No." Alex glared as he inhaled sharply. "*You* decided to force my hand and make me choose between my soulmate and you. She is my everything, and instead of embracing her and welcoming her to the family, you've done everything you can to run her off or turn her into one of us. It doesn't have to be that way."

"Of course, it does." Matthew waved a hand at me. "If she wants to be with you, sacrifices must be made."

"That's not *your* call to make." Alex tucked me behind him and growled, "It's not even mine. It's her decision, and I will respect her choice."

"Matthew, that's enough," Azbogah said. "You're making a scene, and the shifters have done enough."

I glanced over my shoulder to find at least fifty supernaturals standing behind us, gawking.

A group of five caught my attention, their fangs extended and their irises crimson. All five of them stared at me like kids looking at a cake. When our gazes met, they blurred, and it wasn't hard to guess where they were heading.

Time slowed as Alex grabbed my waist and threw me behind him. I flew backward more than twenty feet and landed hard on some rocks, skinning my knees and elbows.

Alex snarled as he threw himself at the three vampires in the center. He leaped and stretched his body lengthwise, knocking them onto their backs and landing on top of them.

Sterlyn and Griffin dropped the panther and raced to me, pure determination etched onto their faces.

I searched for something—anything—to help ward them off. I couldn't count on anyone to save me but myself.

Warm blood dripped down my forearm.

Shit! I had to stop the bleeding.

As if he'd read my mind, someone cool and hard slammed into me, and I fell hard onto my side. Something snapped, and I yelped as pain radiated into my shoulder and down my back.

I must have broken something, but that would be the least of my problems if I didn't get this prick off me.

A hand fisted in my hair, jerking my head to the side. My heart froze, and I tried to fight back, but the person was so much faster and stronger than me. I felt like I was moving sluggishly.

Bracing for the sharp, stabbing pain, I almost cried for joy when the weight was lifted from me. Instead of a biting pain in my neck, my scalp burned as hair was ripped from my skull. My eyes watered, but I'd rather lose hair than have someone drink my blood any day.

"Watch out!" Griffin warned, and I sat upright then cringed as pain shot through my shoulder and chest. The fifth vampire barreled toward me, and I saw drool glistening from the corners of his mouth.

I appreciated the warning, but what was I supposed to do? Throw rocks into his eyes?

Matthew appeared in front of me, blocking the charging vampire.

"Stand down," he shouted, relying on his commanding voice to stop the vampire in his tracks.

I was shocked that he was helping me. Granted, this disaster helped to prove his point that humans didn't belong in Shadow City.

Another argument for another time.

The vampire hesitated, but when his red eyes refocused on me, he blurred at me.

Pain rolled through me, and I feared I would vomit at any second. I couldn't do a damn thing except hope that Matthew would protect me.

Matthew pulled a knife from his waistband, and when the vampire reached us, he slit the guy's throat.

Eyes widening, the vampire gurgled and clamped his hands around his neck. Blood oozed between his fingers and dripped down his green shirt onto the grass. His knees buckled, and he sank to the ground.

A scream caught in my throat. He was dead because of me. Even though I hadn't meant for this to happen, I was partially responsible. I should've stayed in the car.

Huffing, Sterlyn stood over a vampire's dead body, her dagger covered in blood. Griffin's sleeve was tattered with blood oozing through his shirt.

Glad that they were okay, I scanned for Alex. All I saw were three vampire bodies, ripped apart. Alarm buzzed through my chest. "Where's—"

Suddenly, he was beside me. "Are you okay?" His eyes were still red from his vampire fury, but his fangs were shrinking.

"No." I grimaced, hating to appear weak, but the stabbing pain stole my breath. "I...I'm hurt."

Alex's hands automatically went to the injury. He felt around my shoulder, and I grew woozy from the pain.

"Hey," he rasped. "Look at me."

I attempted to listen but couldn't see through my tears.

He gripped my shoulder and arm and jerked. I screamed as pain ripped through my body, but after a loud pop, the pain eased completely.

Breathing became easier, but tears poured down my cheeks. "What did you do?"

"Your shoulder was dislocated. I had to pop it back into place." He pulled me into his arms gently. "I'm so sorry I hurt you."

"Don't be." I moved my arm slowly, afraid the pain would come back. It was sore, but nothing like before. "It's not hurting like it was." I buried my face in his chest, feeling safe in his arms.

He kissed the top of my head. "I was scared I was going to lose you."

A piece of me calmed from his touch. "I'm right here."

"I will bring up this little travesty to the council when we reconvene." Azbogah scowled at the scene before him. "See the havoc her mere presence causes?" He marched to the crowd still gathered on the sidewalk. "Everyone, move on. There is nothing to see here."

Pulling away from Alex, I surveyed the area. I couldn't get past the amount of blood and gore. Was that a detached arm? Bile inched up my throat, and I swallowed, desperate to keep it at bay. The last thing I needed was to vomit in front of Matthew and Azbogah when they were certain I didn't belong here.

But maybe they were right.

"I need to help clean this up." That was something I could do, but where did I start?

"No, we're taking you somewhere safe." Alex cupped my face, forcing me to see only his soft blue eyes. "Fights break out in Shadow City all the time. It usually isn't this brutal, but it's bad enough that we have cleaning crews to take care of things like this."

Maybe a fight to the death wasn't completely out of the ordinary? Or he was trying to make me feel better? *Wait. Sterlyn killed a vampire.*

I know. Alex's jaw muscle twitched, but nothing else gave away his stress. *Don't worry. I'll make sure nothing happens to her. She was protecting you.*

"See, Alex." Matthew strolled over to us, ignoring our

moment. He pointed at the dead vampire. "I killed one of our own for her. Do you realize the fallout this will cause? Their families will be upset. They'll want reparations."

"True, but things were getting out of hand. You did what you had to in order to keep control over your race." Azbogah sneered. "Unlike the wolves here." He pivoted to face Griffin and Sterlyn. "Their families will cause problems, but the council will back your decision. Anyone who causes unrest will be handled."

The longer we stayed here, the worse things got.

"Oh, so we should kill anyone who attacks us? Maybe that's the kind of leaders you two want to be, but not me." Veins bulged in Griffin's neck. "I didn't see you killing any of the shifters."

"Because they were *your* people to control." Matthew pointed at the vampires. "And these were mine. Despite the silver wolf killing one of my people, I'm willing to let that slide since she was protecting my brother's soulmate."

Sterlyn wiped the blood from her dagger on the grass and stood. "How kind."

Something sank in. "Uh...guys. Where's the panther?"

CHAPTER SIXTEEN

A lex spun around, searching for the panther.

There was no way he was hiding in plain sight. The guy had gotten away while we'd been fighting, but this was a small city with strict borders. We should be able to find him relatively easily.

Surely.

The events still seemed too convenient, but Matthew wouldn't have had the vampires show up like that in a highly volatile situation. At least, I hoped he wouldn't. They were his people, after all.

"That's unfortunate." Matthew sighed and placed his hands into his pockets, but the corner of his mouth tipped slightly upward.

Azbogah shook his head and rubbed his hands together. "What did you expect from two wolf shifters who can't control the people they represent?"

"You do realize they attacked not only Griffin but you

as well." Sterlyn put her dagger back in its sheath and stood. "Why aren't you more upset?"

"I am." The angel pulled his shoulders back, making him appear taller. "But those people are your responsibility. Had you taken that more seriously, you wouldn't have let them get away."

"Vampires attacked Veronica," Griffin said menacingly. "Where were you when that happened?"

"Staying out of it and letting the vampires handle their people." Azbogah lifted his hands. "Which Matthew and Alex did very well on their own."

"If it weren't for Sterlyn and Griffin, Veronica could've been killed." Alex stepped closer to me as he glanced back at the sidewalk. "I'm thankful they got involved."

He had to be watching to ensure no other vampires appeared. Everyone was now giving us a wide berth, so hopefully, another attack wouldn't happen so soon.

"Why don't I head back to the condo while you all go search for him?" The last thing they needed was for another vampire to attack me. I hated that this attack would be used against me at the next council meeting. The more ammunition Matthew and his allies had, the better the odds of them getting the majority vote.

Since that meeting, I'd been debating back and forth inside my head whether I wanted to become a vampire, but I couldn't land on a decision. As soon as I considered one, all the consequences associated with that choice made me reconsider everything again.

I wanted Alex, but a whole lot was at stake, and I had

to make sure neither of us resented my decision because an entire lifetime, whether it was sixty years or forever, was a long time to feel that way.

Love couldn't overcome everything, and I had a feeling that was true for soulmates, too.

Alex rocked on his heels. "I'll go with you. I don't want to leave you alone, and I have a feeling Sterlyn and Griffin need me to take the car back."

"Won't they need it to find the panther?" Calling the guy "the panther" felt weird, but I had no better option.

Sterlyn tapped her nose. "Nope, we need to follow his scent, which will be easiest on four legs."

Oh, yeah. Even though parts of the supernatural world were second nature to me, some things still weren't obvious in my mind.

"Shouldn't we go inside and talk about this attack before you four take off?" Azbogah crossed his arms. "A lot happened here."

"Which is why we need to find the panther before he gets too far," Griffin said, glaring at the angel.

Sterlyn pulled the keys from her pocket, along with her badge. "Here—you two head back so Ronnie's safe. We'll return as soon as possible." She handed Alex the stuff and turned.

"Can I help?" Alex asked as surprise wafted through our link.

"Of course, you can't," Matthew snapped. "That's wolf business. Vampires shouldn't be involved."

"But they attacked a vampire and an angel, right?" I wanted to see his and Azbogah's reaction, even though I shouldn't have been goading them. I was already on their radar, so I figured I didn't have much to lose. "Shouldn't both vampires and angels be involved in the search?"

"Until you're officially one of us," Azbogah sneered, "it's best that you stay out of our business."

"You do not get to talk to her that way." Alex fisted his hands at his side. "Veronica is my mate, and you'll treat her with respect. She is part of the royal family, whether you or Matthew like it or not."

"We can stand here and argue, or we can get moving." Sterlyn sniffed, ready to track the panther. "Griffin and I will find him." She took off in a jog toward the end of the block.

"Are you going to let your *mate* tell you what to do?" Azbogah chuckled patronizingly.

Griffin didn't miss a beat. "Yep. When she's right, you can't argue, no matter what sex they are." He took off, rushing to catch up with Sterlyn.

The angel frowned deeply, clearly not enthused with Griffin ignoring his insult. He'd wanted to rile the wolf up, irritating me to no end.

What the hell was wrong with these people?

I'd thought sexism was alive and well in the human realm, but damn. This place put a ton of things into perspective, and I loved Sterlyn more for never backing down. Growing up in an environment like this must have been hard. I'd been here for only a couple of weeks, and the derogatory comments were already wearing on my nerves.

"We need to leave." Alex tugged me toward the vehicle.

"Alex, wait," Matthew called and made his way to us. When Azbogah didn't move, Matthew lifted his brow. "Do you mind?"

"Oh, yes." Azbogah cleared his throat, his eyes tense. "I have things to do anyway. We'll need to call a special meeting about what happened."

They were awfully concerned with meetings and protocol. This was bureaucracy at its worst, but this time, I managed to not say it.

Azbogah marched toward the front of the building. "I'll make the essential calls. We might as well move up our meeting about Veronica. She's caused five vampires to die. The longer she's here as a human, the more volatile the situation will become, I'm afraid."

Great, so now my freedom of choice could be eliminated three days sooner than planned. In the grand scheme of things, that didn't change much, but it was still hard to handle.

"No," Alex hissed.

I interlaced my fingers with his and connected, *Let's go back. It's not worth arguing. They won't change their minds.* And that was the sad truth.

"Are you still planning to come to Griffin and Sterlyn's?" I called to Azbogah, wanting to know whether I would have the pleasure of seeing his ugly mug later.

The angel opened the door. "No, I'll see you here. One of us will check in tomorrow. Don't do anything stupid."

Alex growled and tried to stalk after Azbogah, but I didn't let go of his hand.

I connected to him. *We need to leave before another vampire attacks me.*

I wasn't sure if I was relieved or annoyed that I was still emotional enough for our connection to be clear, but at least the negativity was working to our advantage.

You're right, he relented.

We walked to the Navigator, and suddenly, Matthew blurred to Alex.

"Why don't you come home?" Matthew stared at his brother, ignoring me. I might as well have been invisible.

Maybe that was how most vampires acted, but I'd seen the remorse on Sergio's face after he'd attacked me. And the two houseworkers who'd come after me as we'd left had *tried* not to hurt me.

If vampires were intrinsically selfish, why would they feel bad about hurting someone or try not to hurt someone? The answer was their humanity, which Alex had plenty of. Maybe vampires needed a reason to embrace their human instincts. Maybe that was the point of soulmates—a person to help them remain level-headed.

Matthew reminded me of Eilam and Klyn, but not quite as bad. I wondered if he'd lost part of his humanity. Even Gwen had warmed up to me. He'd killed those vampires for me, but I still didn't believe Matthew truly gave a shit about me, which added to my growing questions.

"Absolutely not." Alex crossed his arms. "She was

just attacked by five vampires. I can't risk taking her back to the mansion."

"Another reason why she has to turn, Alex." Matthew fisted his hands. "You have to see that. You're meant to be home with me, not living with wolves, especially a silver one. You know they're meant to protect both sides. Sterlyn befriending you and Veronica could be a ploy to gain control of Shadow Terrace."

"Stop." Alex halted and turned to fully block me from his brother's view. "I'm staying at the Shadow City alpha's condo. I don't care that Sterlyn is a silver wolf. I only care that they protect and care about Veronica."

I leaned around Alex to view Matthew. When he was around, I was so focused on my anger toward the vampire king that I never paid attention to his reactions.

A deep frown marred his face, and his teak-colored irises darkened to a bittersweet chocolate brown. His facial muscles twitched, but I couldn't read his emotions. Was he hurt that he and his brother were fighting, or was he more concerned about how not having Alex by his side would look? I felt some negativity in his presence that I couldn't put my finger on.

"Why don't you ask Veronica who protected her from that last vampire?" Matthew pivoted and gestured at me. "If it weren't for me, she would've been a snack for the vampire I was forced to kill."

"Exactly. You stepped in at the very end." Alex glowered. "Had you helped me from the beginning, they wouldn't have almost gotten to her."

Matthew exhaled, and for the first time, he seemed speechless.

"That's what I thought." Alex wrapped an arm around my shoulders and ushered me to the Navigator.

Matthew said, "I needed you to see."

Oh, shit. This had the potential to go bad.

"Don't worry." Alex opened the passenger door. "I did."

Ready to get away from all this drama, I leapt inside the vehicle. Growing up in the system, I thought I'd seen my fair share of crap, but this was a whole new level.

Alex shut my door and twirled the keys around his finger. If anything, his anger had boiled into rage. He looked like the guy I'd met in Shadow Terrace that first night.

He faced his brother, his smug smile snapping in place. "I want you to know that Veronica isn't the reason things have changed between us." His voice was muffled through the closed door, but I could make out every word.

"Bullshit," Matthew spat.

"Are you done?" Alex asked, his soft blue eyes turning to ice. When Matthew said nothing, he continued, "Things were changing before she got here. You were so focused on the silver wolf and ensuring we kept control of Shadow Terrace that something happened."

"Yes, it did," Matthew snarled. "We have to secure our place in this society by whatever means necessary."

"You're wrong." Alex lifted his hands. "At first, like you, I had concerns. That's why I started collecting favors from Sterlyn, but all we were..." He trailed off, then he pointed at his brother. "You're worried about something that's destroying you. We were so focused on Shadow City and the wolves that we let things get out of control in Shadow Terrace. We let our people lose a part of themselves that they can never get back."

Matthew pointed in the direction of Shadow Terrace. "That was their choice."

"No." Alex wagged a finger. "No, it wasn't. That day in the blood bank, when he was attacking the love of my life, Eilam admitted he'd forced many to turn. We allowed people to run Shadow Terrace for centuries, while we stayed safe behind these walls. We"—he gestured between himself and Matthew—"failed our people and will continue to do so if we forget who we are and let our hatred rule us."

After a pause, Alex nodded and marched toward the driver's side door.

Matthew blurred, and I screamed, but not fast enough to warn him.

CHAPTER SEVENTEEN

Matthew shoved Alex against the Navigator so hard that the car shook. He might have even made a dent, but the vampire king didn't care.

"Do not forget who you are talking to," Matthew breathed so low I barely could hear. "I am your king, and I will never fail my people."

"Believe what you have to in order to sleep well at night." Alex pushed his brother off him, not bowing to the threat. "You're spiraling and becoming obsessive over the potential silver wolf threat. And that obsession could not only become detrimental to our people but the city as a whole."

Alex could finally see the truth for what it was. Matthew's blind hatred for others outside their own race was bad for everyone, especially where the wolves were concerned.

"This is what our relationship has become." Matthew

patted his chest and gestured to Alex as he rasped, "The spare taking on the king, wanting the crown for himself."

"What? No!" Alex's mouth dropped. "Why in the *hell* would you think that? I've never wanted to rule, and you know it."

"That used to be the case." Matthew's glare turned on me. "But that was before *she* came into the picture."

Alex's jaw clenched, and his chest heaved. "I do not desire to be king. Protecting my mate and having people's best interests at heart is what *I* care about."

Matthew gasped. "And you don't think I do?"

The answer to that was obvious, and I agreed with Alex. Matthew wasn't focused on anything besides making the wolves look bad and forcing me to turn. Every other issue had fallen to the wayside.

"You've essentially locked me in the city." Alex's nose creased. "I can't follow up on who was working with Eilam while I'm in here. Who knows if humans are still being drained and vampires are still losing their humanity? Have you checked in with Shadow Terrace?"

Matthew's pale face turned a shade of pink.

I was pretty sure his skin tone would change to that color permanently. Good thing he was immortal, or he'd have severe blood pressure issues. Wait...could vampires have high blood pressure? I was still naïve about so much of this.

"I never said you couldn't leave." Matthew nodded toward me. "Only her until the council has come to an agreement and executed that decision."

If that hadn't been a "she's going to turn" kind of

comment, I wasn't sure what else it could be. He was determined to make sure the council had no choice but to turn me.

"Not allowing her to leave is the same thing as not allowing me to leave. I won't leave her alone in this city, not with you working against us." Alex raised his hands in frustration. "You should know that! And if you don't, then you're not nearly as smart as I thought."

Matthew laughed cruelly. "But she wouldn't be alone. Right? Your best friends, Griffin and Sterlyn, would watch after her. Or are they only friends when it benefits you?"

With the amount of glee on his face, Matthew sure thought he'd made a good point. But Alex's desire to stay with me wasn't a reflection of how he felt about the wolves. It was about us being soulmates. If I'd felt like he was in danger, I wouldn't leave his side either. Besides, I trusted Sterlyn with my life.

"And that's the point." Alex deflated, all the anger leaving him. "We've been trapped in this city for so long that we've forgotten what having a soulmate means. Even Shadow Terrace residents weren't allowed to leave the perimeter, so it's been decades since many of them found someone to love."

"Oh, you mean a human soulmate?" Matthew took a jerky step backward. "I'd say it's a good thing we haven't found them."

"You know that's not true." Alex sighed. "Mom and Dad were soulmates who happened to live in the same city and were both born vampires. I don't know why I'm mated to a human, but that's rare, and you know it. But the world outside these walls has exploded. Soulmates are out there—we just have to give our people permission to leave so fate can help them find each other."

"Fate would bring them here if they were out there." Mathew grunted. "Like your human. Besides, if we released the vampires from inside the city, they would feast on humans, since they've never had to fight those urges before."

I should have kept my mouth shut, but the longer I sat here, the harder it was. "Maybe I was brought here to help you all see the bigger picture and point things out," I called through the car door. "The university, for instance. It could design and offer classes to teach vampires how to control those urges. Fate finally intervened."

"She always has to interject." Matthew gestured at me. "Doesn't she realize—"

"That she has a voice and I love to hear what she thinks?" Alex arched his brow. "And that because of her, I'm finally seeing things as they are? Be careful what you say, dear brother, because you keep fracturing *our* relationship."

Unexpectedly, that shut Matthew up. He closed his eyes and lifted his head skyward, trying to remain calm. "I hate that our relationship has come to this."

His statement sounded like a veiled threat, and that didn't sit well with me. I wanted to punch the arrogant son of a bitch.

Remain calm, Alex connected, pushing reassurance at me. *I've been falling into his trap for too long, and we have to be smarter than him.* Despite communicating with me, his gaze remained locked on his brother. "Me too."

Matthew exhaled as he rolled his shoulders. "Very well. But remember, she is not allowed to leave until the council makes their final decision and that you saw the shifters attack us with your own eyes. Since you have such integrity, keep that in mind when our meeting takes place." He paused, waiting for Alex's reaction.

"Of course." Alex nodded. "I will speak the truth."

"Good." Matthew patted his shoulder then glared at me once more with hatred.

Unease coursed through me, but I refused to shiver, wishing to avoid letting him see my reaction, emotional or physical. What was it with assholes trying to intimidate everyone? People like Azbogah and Matthew did it with each other, but they went over the top when dealing with me, Sterlyn, or any female, really.

Alex climbed into the Navigator and shut the door calmly. Anger rolled off him, but he gave the perception of confidence and coolness.

"You know—" I started.

He started the car and hissed, "Shh."

Oh, hell no. "Excuse you." I couldn't believe he'd shushed me. He wasn't my parent.

He can still hear you. Alex pulled out of the parking spot without looking behind him. "Let's get you back to the condo."

Ah, supernatural hearing. I stayed quiet as he pulled onto the main road, heading toward Sterlyn's.

"Are we safe now?" I asked, keeping the question

vague so Matthew would think I meant from vampires if he could still hear us.

Glancing in the rearview mirror, he chuckled. "Yeah, we're good."

That brought to mind something that would be beneficial for me to know. "Who all has extra-good hearing?"

His face brightened in a way that made me smile in return. "In general, all supernaturals. Our magic causes it. Shifters have the best hearing, except for birds. The bird shifters have the best sight in the right conditions."

"What does that mean?" I turned so I could enjoy staring at his profile. His shirt hugged his chest just right so I could see the contours of his athletic frame, and my mind flashed to his body moving over mine earlier today.

Whoa. Down, girl.

"For instance, falcons have excellent sight during the day, but at night, they're impaired." He tapped his fingers on the steering wheel as he scanned the area more intensely than usual.

He must have been searching for the panther in case he was blending in with the surroundings. I could do that too. I tore my gaze away from him and scanned the streets, focusing on shadowed nooks and around corners. "Are there all kinds of bird shifters?"

"There is only a handful—falcons, crows, hawks, eagles, and ravens—and every bird in the city is a shifter because only supernatural creatures live here. It can get complicated outside of Shadow City."

"I've been meaning to ask—why do only wolves

represent shifters on the council? I'd expect there to be a representative for every race."

"That's where Sterlyn's heritage comes into play." Alex glanced at me. "The original council refused to let every shifter have a representative because then that species would have the most influence. Even though they are different races and stick to themselves, they have over-arching interests. The point of the council was to keep the balance where no majority bias was evident. The one race every shifter trusted was the silver wolf because they were born to protect every supernatural race. A shifter vote was cast, and the silver wolves were appointed as the shifter representatives."

Sterlyn did have everyone's best interests at heart. "They made a wise decision."

"Two months ago, I'd have been hesitant to agree, but I meant what I told Matthew. You opened my eyes." Alex squeezed my thigh before focusing back on our surroundings. "The silver wolves left the city before the very first council meeting, but the decision couldn't be undone, so the alpha of the Shadow City pack, his beta, and his third in command took their spots."

"With the silver wolves gone, is that why the vampires guard one side of the river and Killian's pack the other?" Things were starting to make a little more sense. "And the council started up as originally intended?"

"The first answer is yes. Killian's ancestor's pack wasn't big enough or strong enough, like the silver wolves, to protect both sides of the river. Since vampires needed a way to get blood inside the city, and are strong fighters and trackers too, it was logical for us to control the other side."

A lightbulb went off in my head. "That's why the vampires are worried the wolves will take over, especially since Sterlyn is back."

"Yeah." Alex ran his hand along the steering wheel. "I was concerned, too. I didn't want to get to know her and only thought the worst."

"Hey, you were biased." We were all guilty of that. When I was growing up, a lot of people pegged me as the stereotypical foster kid who was up to no good even though I was a rule follower. "But you realize it now and have opened your mind. I'm so proud of you, and—" I kissed his cheek. "—I find that very sexy."

"Oh, well." His eyes lightened back to the soft, warm blue I loved. "Then let me also tell you I thought all humans were stupid."

"And?" I bit my bottom lip.

He leaned over the center console and whispered, "I was right."

"You jerk!" I squealed, playfully punching him in the arm. "How dare you!"

"Oh, stop." He took my hand. "You know I'm kidding."

"Ha ha." I stuck out my tongue at him, my nervousness from what we'd gone through completely gone.

He turned down the road to the condo. "But to answer your earlier question, the angels took control of the city, which is why it changed from a safe haven to a place where only the strongest of each supernatural race live. The angels wanted to rule over all supernaturals, and so they enticed families with riches and a place that resembled Heaven, making it a competition to live here. When the angels became too demanding, the silver wolves organized all the races and banded them together to take the angels down. We learned we could overcome the angels when we all worked together. When the angels fell, the city's borders were shut so we could clean up the mess inside, and that's when the council was formed."

"And the city stayed shut for centuries?" That part was surprising.

As we reached the gate of the underground parking lot, he slowed and pulled out Sterlyn's badge. "When a group works together to overcome a common enemy and the enemy falls, everything fractures. We finally realized that the city would never be perfect and we were hurting ourselves by staying closed off. Griffin's father, Atticus, hoped that opening the border would bring the supernaturals together."

"Which it has not." It was funny how things went sometimes.

"No." The gate opened, and Alex drove through. "It created different problems, but closing the city again isn't a good solution. Still, only a select few are allowed in and out, and they aren't granting more access. Azbogah demands that until we see the people integrate back into the world successfully, no one else should leave, though technically, a council member can grant any of their people the right to go outside. People are afraid of the angels, though, so no one has asked to leave. The damage is done. It's like we're stagnant."

I agreed. "We have to change that, but we have to handle the most pressing issues first. I want to get back to supernatural hearing." I was over talking about the council and its problems.

"After shifters, vampires and angels have the best hearing." We coasted into the bottom of the lot, and he continued, "No one knows why, but they're basically on par. And last are the witches. They can hear better than humans, but without the aid of their magic, not much better. Witches, though, can travel outside their bodies to eavesdrop. You can feel a chill in the air when they do that if you're paying attention."

Good to know. "I don't feel a chill from the shadow."

"Have you seen it again?" he asked tensely as he cruised into Griffin's parking spot.

There was no point in lying. "I thought I saw it next to Azbogah earlier. Then I got attacked. When I looked again, the shadow was gone. I don't know if I imagined it."

"If something evil was going to follow anyone, it would definitely be that asshole." Alex shifted into Park harder than necessary. "Unfortunately, I think that goes for my brother, too."

I hated that he felt that way, but I couldn't disagree. Those two were working together, and Matthew's demeanor turned malicious each time I ran into him. "Let's go inside and try to relax."

We proceeded to the elevator, and I leaned my head on his shoulder the entire ride up. Alex slipped his fingers under my shirt, and my body warmed.

I would never tire of him. I faced him, standing on my tiptoes to kiss his lips. He responded immediately, his tongue sliding inside my mouth. His sweet flavor washed over me.

After a crappy day, I was desperate for one type of relaxation. I pressed against him, and he hardened.

The doors opened, but Alex didn't pull away. Instead, he grabbed my ass and lifted me so I could wrap my legs around his waist.

What if Ulva's home? I protested weakly, somewhat aware of our surroundings.

Instead of pulling away, he walked down the hallway on a mission. *We're alone. Thank God.*

Within seconds, he was slamming the door to our room and pressing my back to the wall, making me moan and writhe against him.

I slid down his body, relishing the feel of him, and put my feet on the ground. I unfastened his pants and pushed them off him in desperation.

"Slow down," he growled as he lifted my shirt over my head and unfastened my bra. He stepped back, drinking me in. Instead of covering myself, I stood proudly and let him see how much I wanted him.

He was the only person in the world who made me feel sexy, and I had a feeling that would never change. Wanting to see him as well, I tugged his shirt over his head and tossed it onto the floor. I ran my hands over his smooth skin, enjoying the cool, smooth feel of his hard chest.

Holding his gaze, I pulled off my pants and underwear and stepped out of them. We stood naked in front of each other.

"Veronica." My name sounded like a plea. He lowered his head and captured my nipple in his mouth, and he slipped a hand between my legs.

The onslaught of sensation mixed with emotions overtook me. He nipped and circled, hitting both spots exactly the way I liked it. My body heated, and I threw my head back against the wall, crazed with hunger.

Pushing his hand away, I arched my back, making it clear what I wanted.

He hoisted me against him again and entered me in one move, filling me completely.

Our bodies moved together as he thrust in and out, increasing the friction. I never wanted it to end.

In this moment, only the two of us existed in the world.

His back muscles contracted under my hands, the power turning me on even more.

He kissed down my neck and nipped at the base. I wanted to beg him to bite me, but he always seemed uneasy, afraid to hurt me. I knew he'd never purposely hurt me, but he was a vampire.

I increased our rhythm, digging my nails into his back. He groaned in ecstasy and pumped inside me harder.

Our connection opened, our pleasure blending. As

his body released, the intense emotion pushed me over the top. We orgasmed as one, and our bodies stilled, leaving our harsh breathing the only sound in the room.

"You are amazing, and I'm so damn lucky." He brushed his lips against mine and sighed. "I'd love to go for another round, but we better get dressed and get out there before Sterlyn and Griffin return."

I hated that our moment was over, but he was right. We had pressing things to address.

Once we were dressed, we headed into the main room, still expecting to be alone. Instead, I found Sterlyn, Griffin, and Rosemary in the living room. My cheeks heated. Could they tell what we'd done?

But no one so much as blinked at us. Rosemary's face was lined with concern, and Griffin paced the room. He seemed angry. Sterlyn stood at the glass doors, staring out at the city. The tension was so thick I could barely breathe.

"What's going on?" They needed to spit out whatever had happened.

CHAPTER EIGHTEEN

No one said anything as Alex and I joined them in the room.

For them to have returned so quickly, they must have found the panther. "Where's the guy?" I didn't know his name, so "the guy" it would be.

"Hiding," Rosemary said. She pulled her hair up into a bun, which I'd never seen her do.

Alex started with surprise. "Then why are you here?"

"Because we'd be wasting our time searching for him." Sterlyn turned from the sliding door and leaned against the glass. "He's a black panther and can outrun us, especially over long distances. Besides, we're certain the attackers had an exit strategy and a hiding place set up, so there wasn't any point in looking for them without more information."

"Can't you sniff them out?" Next time Alex and I talked, I'd ask about supernatural smelling abilities.

Griffin's pacing increased. "We tracked the panther

for a mile, but he vanished. The shifters who attacked us likely had a spell or chemical to hide their scents. That's why Rosemary is here. She did a flyover of the entire dome and saw nothing out of the ordinary."

That sounded on par with our luck lately. "But you know who it was, right?" Any sort of lead would be better than a dead end.

"Yes, but we have to be careful since the panther's family is influential. If we accuse him or act against him without proof, it will only fuel the council's determination to mess with Ronnie and Alex." Griffin stilled. "And if it's who I think it is, he's a good guy. I'm thinking he wasn't trying to hurt anyone. I want to find him to figure out who the hell this group is working with."

"I didn't sense any vileness from him, and he was standing at the back of the shifters at the council building riot. But I didn't get a strong scent from anyone." Sterlyn rubbed her fingers together as if that helped her think. "I'm assuming their clothes and masks were spelled to hide their individual scents. I couldn't smell the panther until we'd removed his mask."

So, we had a good guy wrapped up in something shady.

I hated being the one who kept asking questions, but I wanted to be helpful. "So, a witch is working with them?" Figured. That Erin woman was a hot mess filled with so much hatred. She and Azbogah reminded me of Eilam.

"No, not necessarily." Rosemary sat on the couch. "Witches barter all the time, so it's easy to access that kind of magic. The younger generations like to use scent-masking spells to prank their parents or teachers or whatever, so we can't go accusing the witches of anything without—" She paused chuckling. "—causing more problems with the council."

Holy shit. "What *can* we do?"

"Our hands are tied." Griffin nibbled on his lip. "Unless we get a break."

Alex led me to the couch opposite Rosemary, and we sat down together. "They want you to look as inept as possible."

"But I don't see shifters willingly working with Azbogah and Matthew." Sterlyn sighed. "We're missing something."

"Unless they're making it worth their while." Rosemary leaned forward, placing her elbows on her thighs.

Griffin shook his head. "Shifters know not to trust a vampire." He grimaced and glanced at Alex. "With the exception of you now."

Alex laughed and placed an arm around my shoulders. "That's the nicest thing you've ever said to me, and you're right. You can only trust vampires if we owe you a favor, and even then, we look for loopholes. My brother goes out of his way not to owe anyone. It's a game for him. He doesn't want his ass on the line, especially with shifters. Either someone is working with them on my brother's behalf, or it's something else entirely." He pulled out his phone and began typing. "I'll message Gwen and see if she's heard anything."

"Will she tell you the truth?" Griffin frowned. "You might alert Matthew of our suspicions."

"No, she's safe," Sterlyn said, placing a hand on her mate's shoulder. "She's lost some of her malice, similar to Alex, whereas Matthew is spiraling down a bad path."

"Tell me something I don't know." Alex rolled his eyes and pressed send. "But yes, after all of you helped Veronica save her, her perspective changed. She knows none of you had to help or protect her, yet each one of you did without hesitation. It's hard for us to understand that people like that exist in the world, since most vampires are selfish by nature. Even when it comes to family, it can be a struggle to put someone before yourself, and not many do."

"I understand that." Rosemary leaned back in her seat, watching us with eyes that were a dark purple. "Even though angels technically have humanity, we're more angel than human. The story is that we were given a small amount of human empathy to distinguish right from wrong, but our supernatural nature—our strongest side—tries to ignore the emotions, so we often seem cold and heartless."

"But not selfish," Griffin said.

"If we don't completely ignore our humanity, we can sense when something isn't right and consider the greater good. Of course, there are two extremes—one in which an angel embraces their human side, which I've been doing more and more since getting involved with the silver wolves, and another in which they turn away from it completely."

"Like Azbogah." He seemed heartless.

"Believe it or not, he truly believes he has the angels' best interest in mind. His actions are borderline unethical, but he can justify it in his own demented way." Rosemary shivered.

Sterlyn laid her head on Griffin's shoulder. "If he hasn't turned away from his humanity, I'd hate to see an angel who has."

Rosemary shifted in her seat, indicating she wanted to drop the conversation.

I decided to assist her since she always respected my boundaries. "What are our next steps? The council is calling another meeting in two days to discuss the attacks and decide my fate."

"What?" Griffin growled.

I'd forgotten that conversation had occurred after they'd left. Maybe that had been on purpose.

"Yeah." Alex hugged me closer. "They're giving you today and tomorrow to determine who attacked us and why."

"In other words, they're hoping we'll fail." Sterlyn straightened as tension rolled off her. "I wish I could get Cyrus and the silver wolves here to help."

She rarely mentioned the other silver wolves. "Why can't they?"

"Outsiders aren't allowed in the city yet. You and I are the exceptions because we're mated to council members." Sterlyn looped her arm through Griffin's. "And everyone is uncomfortable with my presence here, so bringing in more silver wolves would only cause more panic. Besides that, my brother is new to the alpha role and getting the silver wolves settled into their new neighborhood. Until we know it's safe, it's best if we keep them off the grid. I'd hate to bother him with the stuff going on here. But if things get worse, we may not have a choice."

"It should be a last resort," Griffin agreed. "Because the guards won't let them through the gates, and we'd risk going up against most of the council to authorize it."

Rosemary undid her bun, letting her gorgeous mahogany hair fall past her shoulders. "Mom and Dad will side with you."

"As will Gwen and I," Alex said as his phone dinged.

"That's the problem." Sterlyn walked back to gaze out of the door to the balcony. "The council is divided. Ezra would go along with us, so we'd have enough votes, but we'd only fracture the relationships even more."

Alex exhaled as he read the message. "Gwen couldn't find out anything from her connections, either. It's unlikely that Matthew or another vampire orchestrated the attack."

"Which is what we figured." Griffin tapped his fingers against his jeans. "Did anyone notice anything that might hint at who is involved?"

After a pause, Sterlyn groaned. "No. I was so concerned with getting to you that I didn't pay attention like I normally do."

"Hey, it's not your fault." Griffin pulled her into his arms and kissed the top of her head. "Now you know what I went through every time you were in danger."

"Yeah, it's harder than I realized," Sterlyn admitted dejectedly.

Rosemary's gaze landed on Alex. "What about you?"

It bothered me that she'd disregarded me, but I had to remember it wasn't personal. I didn't have heightened senses like the rest of them.

"No." He caressed my shoulder. "I was focused on Sterlyn and her driving. She was reckless, at first, while getting to Griffin."

The redheaded girl popped into my head. "This probably isn't relevant, but I noticed a group of people about two blocks down from the council building, looking that way."

I had everyone's attention, which made me feel a little uncomfortable.

Sterlyn smiled encouragingly. "Anyone catch your eye?"

"Yeah, there was this short girl with bright red hair—" I started, but a loud knock at the door interrupted me.

Everyone stilled, and an even louder knock pounded on the door.

"Are you guys expecting someone?" Rosemary whispered softly enough that I almost couldn't hear.

Griffin frowned. "No one should be up here. I'll get it." He started for the door, grumbling about having a talk with building security.

"Here." Sterlyn removed her dagger from her ankle sheath and jumped up to hand it to him. "We can't be too careful."

He nodded and clutched it to his chest.

A conversation went on between them that none of us could hear. They had to be using their mate connection, same as Alex and I did.

Sterlyn followed her mate, not comfortable with him opening the door alone.

The rest of us stayed in the living room on the edge of our seats. I wasn't sure what to expect. Azbogah had stated he wouldn't be coming here.

My heart pounded, and I hoped we weren't about to face another attack. Fate had to give us a break.

"Why is Kira here?" Alex's forehead lined with confusion, and something in his voice made me examine him closely.

"Uh...should I know her?"

"No, she's a fox shifter," he answered and squeezed my arm gently.

Rosemary shrugged and remained silent.

Footsteps headed toward us. "Should I say thanks for not stabbing me?" a girlish voice I'd never heard before asked.

"Yeah, you should," Griffin growled. "How the hell did you get up here? The front desk shouldn't have let you in without announcing you."

"You underestimate me." She laughed. "I know about the secret staircase meant for emergencies. I thought this constituted an emergency. I used it so I wouldn't alert anyone to my presence."

I glanced over my shoulder as the very girl I'd just mentioned entered the living room with Griffin and Sterlyn right behind her.

"That's her." I probably sounded dazed, but I couldn't get over the fact that she was standing here with us. "That's the girl I noticed on the way to the council building."

Her emerald eyes focused on me as she strolled toward the sizable glass windows overlooking the city. She tossed her red hair over her shoulder, and when Rosemary stood and towered over her, I realized how small she was. She was shorter than me, which was saying something in the supernatural world.

"It's a damn good thing I came here of my own free will, then." One hand propped up her chin as her attention stayed on me. "Otherwise, you might not be so willing to work with me."

Alex's jaw twitched. "What the hell does that mean?"

"And why were you watching the attack?" Sterlyn scanned the girl as if searching for something inside her. "Do you know something about it?"

"Good questions." Kira crossed her arms, causing her black shirt, which was a lovely contrast against her beige-gold complexion, to tighten around her waist. "And I intend to answer them."

She'd been here less than a minute and was already getting on my nerves. Who the hell did she think she was, coming here with a cocky smirk on her face, playing some sort of game? It reminded me of the way the group home wardens would act when a punishment was about to be doled out. The longer they kept it secret, the more powerful they felt. I couldn't hide my irritation. "What's the catch?"

The girl observed me with complete amusement, her eyes sparkling. "The human actually has the nerve to speak."

"If you don't start talking, fox, you won't find this funny much longer," Alex growled, and annoyance wafted through our bond.

Griffin huffed. "The more Alex and I are around each other, the more we think alike." He lifted the dagger and twirled it between his hands.

"You idiots don't scare me." She waved them off and looked at each one of us, taking her time. "You already have your hands full. The last thing you need is another enemy."

Sterlyn batted her eyes. "You're here because you're concerned for us. Aw, that's sweet."

The fox's face fell. "Don't be sarcastic. I have information you can use."

"Then please, blow our minds." Alex's words were laced with humor, but his fingers had stiffened on my arm. Unease flowed through our bond, but if he hadn't been touching me and I hadn't been connected to him, I never would've known.

"Sure, I can do that." She winked at him, making my blood boil.

Irrational jealousy consumed me. That bitch better watch herself around him. He was mine, and I'd pee on him to prove it. Wait...I knew animals peed to mark their territory. Did the same thing go for shifters? If so, I was game. *One more flirty gesture and you're getting a golden shower.*

The expression that crossed his face was priceless. His face wrinkled, and his eyes cut to me. *What is a golden shower? It sounds nice, but I'm thinking it isn't.*

Bless his heart. *Pee. I'm going to pee on you.*

If that makes you...happy ... His face scrunched like he'd sucked a lemon. *I guess—*

Whoa. He thought I was into that. What the hell? *I mean like a dog pees on things to mark its territory.*

Oh, thank goodness. A cocky smirk spread on his face. *Oh...I like you jealous, but you have absolutely nothing to worry about.*

I know that. I wasn't worried about Alex. Kira could strip down to her bra and panties, and my mate would only have eyes for me. But I didn't want *her* thinking of him like that.

"Please," Rosemary snapped, waving a hand at the newcomer. "Awe us with your knowledge."

"I will, but I need something guaranteed first." She tilted her head back. "Nothing in life is free."

CHAPTER NINETEEN

"And here I thought vampires were bad," Griffin muttered. "We're shifters, just like you, and three of us are council members. Are you sure trying to blackmail us is wise?"

"Yup." Kira popped the 'p,' adding to her impression of arrogance. "Because if you don't, you won't be council members much longer." Another smirk flitted over her face.

She'd said those words with so much conviction that they were hard to ignore. Something about her both intrigued and infuriated me. She had so much more to her below the surface.

Sterlyn chuckled. "And why is that? Because Azbogah and Matthew are trying to make us appear like we aren't in control?"

"Maybe they aren't the problem." Kira shrugged and glanced at the city. "But who knows?"

Shit, could she have been listening outside our door?

That didn't seem plausible. There had to be measures in place to ensure people couldn't eavesdrop, especially if all the bedrooms were soundproofed, but maybe only the bedrooms were soundproofed and not the entire condo.

"Why don't you just say it, or I'll beat it from you?" Rosemary threatened, stalking toward the fox shifter.

Kira didn't flinch or turn to look at the angry angel. She leaned a forearm against the glass. "You won't beat me, even if you want to, because then Azbogah will have leverage over your parents, and we both know he's been *desperately* searching for some."

The wind left Rosemary as her shoulders slumped.

Corruption was everywhere. This place was no different from the outside world, other than it being more violent and volatile.

"Let's hear her out," Alex said as he laid his hand in my lap. "I bet she doesn't know much."

Kira snorted. "Nice strategy. That would work on a male set out to prove himself, but I don't fall for those games. You either want the information I have, or you don't."

Threats wouldn't work with her. This negotiation would have to be more logical. I glanced at Sterlyn, who nodded as if we had a mental link. Of course, we didn't, but I had a feeling we'd reached the same conclusion.

"Fine, we might be willing to negotiate with you, but we need proof that you have valuable information first," Sterlyn said as she strolled to the couch and sat on my other side.

Yup, we had reached the same conclusion. Maybe I could integrate into this world eventually.

"*That* I'm willing to work with." Kira spun around to face everyone in the room again. "I'm willing to drop half of what I know on you as long as you can promise that if my information is useful, the two of you"—she nodded to Griffin and Sterlyn—"will back me to take over leadership of the foxes upon my father's retirement in the next few months."

Rosemary's breath hitched. "Your dad is stepping down?"

Kira cut her eyes to the angel. "Yes, though it's not public knowledge."

"Why should we get involved?" Griffin cocked his head. "He's the one who decides who inherits his role, so you're a shoo-in."

She laughed without humor, pain flashing in her eyes. "You'd think that was the case, but no. My entire life, I've done everything to prove that, despite being female, I would make the best leader. But it wasn't enough. He plans to back my cousin, his eldest nephew, as his replacement."

"Of course." The sexism seemed to be over the top here.

"In the shifter world, men are usually stronger physically, and for some reason, our society equates that with being the best leader." Sterlyn frowned. "Believe me, Dad pushed me harder than any of the boys he trained to make sure I could stand my ground against anyone who challenged me."

"At least, you had a supportive dad." Kira's tone held bitterness.

"Wait...he wants *Grady* to succeed him?" Griffin grimaced. "That guy is a tool."

"Right." Kira sighed, her expression smoothing as if she'd needed the validation. "And if I don't get backing from the council, he will take over."

I scanned the group to see how they were processing the information. Alex was intrigued, I knew that from our connection, but I was clueless about the others. Sterlyn and Griffin stared at each other, using their mate connection to discuss things, while Rosemary stared at the fox with interest. The angel's eyes narrowed as if the fox were a puzzle she was trying to piece together.

"We'll need a second to discuss this." Sterlyn stood and waved her hand at our group. "This isn't a decision one of us can make alone since it impacts us all."

Kira's eyebrows shot up before her face smoothed back into indifference. "Should I leave?"

"Nope." Griffin gestured for us to follow him. "Stay here. We can talk in my office."

I expected Kira to say something snarky like, "You aren't my alpha," or something along those lines, but she only nodded and turned back toward the skyline.

That told me everything I needed to know. I'd played the same game with the wardens back in the day. She was as desperate for our help as we were for hers, and she was doing everything she could to seem blasé. Her hands shook before she clasped them in front of her, confirming my suspicions.

The five of us marched down the hallway, straight to the room I'd never seen anyone enter.

Griffin hesitated before opening the door and leading us inside.

Just like the other rooms, the outer walls were all glass. The view of the city was breathtaking with the swirls of color dancing outside and reflecting off the various metal and white buildings. The wall that backed to the hallway was dark charcoal with a muted gray fireplace taking up the wall that bordered Griffin and Sterlyn's room.

A massive slate-colored wooden desk occupied the center of the room with various notebooks stacked in rows. Griffin sat in the mammoth black leather office chair and placed his forearms on the desk. "What are you all thinking?"

"One thing we know for sure; we don't want that idiot Grady leading the foxes." Alex motioned as if a bomb had exploded in his brain. "That guy is a loose cannon."

Griffin chuckled. "Again, I have to agree with you there. But she knows we all feel that way, so why would she hold that over our heads? Something doesn't feel right about it."

"And that's where it's obvious you aren't a woman." Even in the human world, women and many other minorities suffered these types of inherent biases.

"Babe?" Alex stepped closer to me, his chest brushing against mine. "You know there is nothing feminine about me."

"I'm not even as human as the four of you, and I knew that one of these alphaholes would have to make some sort of dick comment," Rosemary scoffed as she pushed her hair back. "Which tells you how damn predictable you are."

I laughed, which felt weird, given the circumstances, but she'd pegged them so perfectly.

Sterlyn patted Alex's back like he was a small child. "What Ronnie was saying is that most women, especially those who grew up in homes like Kira's, would never fathom a male willingly backing them. She assumes she has to hold something over your heads to get you to agree to put her in a position of power."

"No way," Griffin said with disbelief and rolled back in the chair. "We have Rosemary's mom, you, Gwen, and an entire coven on the council."

"But Mom constantly has to prove herself, not only to Azbogah and the other angels, but to herself." Rosemary glanced at the slate-gray carpet. "Or how Matthew—and let's be honest, at one time, Alex—ignores most of Gwen's suggestions if they conflict with his views."

"And don't forget that Dick and the others were desperate to get me to leave." Sterlyn walked behind Griffin and placed her hands on his shoulders. "It's not like they rolled out the red carpet for me."

"Only the witches hold their own, but that's because they're the one race where women are naturally stronger than men," Rosemary added. "The women haven't had it easy here."

I almost felt bad for the guys. Alex bit his bottom lip

as he contemplated our words.

Griffin exhaled and said, "You're right. In some ways, the city being closed off for so long slowed our progress."

"True, but it's not just that." Sterlyn placed her chin on Griffin's head. "Our culture values strength. That's how we do things. If you want an alpha role, you challenge the current alpha. Whoever wins gets the pack. It's also how we were built. But the thing is, women have their own strength. For instance, when I fight, even as a silver wolf, I use my size to my advantage."

This was a good conversation that could last for hours, if not days, but that wasn't what we were here to discuss. "If you guys want Kira to take over the position, I say we agree and find out what she knows."

"What if she doesn't know anything?" Alex rubbed a hand over his mouth. "We would be agreeing to something without getting anything in return."

"We tell her that she has to tell us something useful, and once we've verified it, we'll agree. Then she should tell us all she knows." Sterlyn shifted her weight to one leg. "That way we should get some useful information."

"Or she sets us up to look worse than we already do in a last-ditch effort to win her father's favor." Griffin stood and shuffled through the notebooks.

He opened the first one, and a dust cloud exploded.

I inhaled a mouthful and coughed. "How long has it been since anyone cleaned in here?"

He shrugged. "No clue."

I waved a hand in front of my face to clear the dust motes.

"We should chance it." Sterlyn lifted her hands. "I don't think we'll get any leads fast enough otherwise. She could be our best hope."

"We could always do some fact-checking. We can ask her various questions to trip her up and catch her in a lie." Rosemary pursed her lips. "If she reeks, we don't act on it."

"If this can put off the council meeting and give us more time to figure out an alternative for Veronica, I say we try it." Alex jabbed a finger in the air. "We're both running out of time."

"Is that what everyone thinks?" Griffin asked and scanned the room.

Even though I wasn't an official supernatural, I spoke anyway. "Yeah, I agree."

"Fine, but don't promise her anything." Griffin slammed the notebook shut and marched to the door. "If anyone begins to have doubts, alert the group."

They'd made me feel like an important member of the group, and my heart was so full it could burst.

As we entered the living room, Kira turned around eagerly. She took a deep breath and licked her lips. I sat on the couch with Alex on one side and Rosemary on the other.

Griffin stood behind our couch, and Sterlyn approached Kira wearily.

"Is this a move to gain your father's approval?" Sterlyn asked bluntly.

Kira smiled and tilted her head. "I would do something like that, but in this case, I am not." She stared

Sterlyn in the eye. "This is not a ploy to get the upper hand. I'm offering a mutually beneficial agreement."

"She's not lying," Rosemary stated.

I didn't have their super senses, but I felt a bond with Kira. Even though she had a father, it was clear he wasn't the best, and she hadn't mentioned her mother, so who knew the story there. I understood what it felt like to have a home where you didn't feel accepted. "Tell us what you know."

"Your little pet is pretty cocky, acting as if she's a legitimate part of your group." Kira chuckled.

Alex sneered. "She isn't my pet. She's my *mate,* and she is a part of this group. She helped bring us together."

She snorted, but it fell short when she realized no one disagreed with him. Her expression sobered, and she gasped.

"You heard what she said." Sterlyn pointed at me, backing me up.

"I did." Kira pulled on her shirt and scratched her brow. "I won't spill everything I know, but I'll tell you a little bit, and once you back me, I'll fill in the rest."

"That's not—" Griffin started.

"Fine." Kira strolled toward the door. "Those are my terms. Take it or leave it."

Sterlyn growled, "Just tell us the first half, and if it pans out, we'll back you after you've told us everything."

The fox stopped and smiled smugly. "There's a shifter in your midst who organized today's attacks. It wasn't a vampire or an angel."

They'd already been thinking that, so Kira might

legitimately know something. Maybe we would actually get ahead of someone for once.

Griffin waved his hand. "Who is it?"

"I don't know." Kira's shoulders deflated.

Alex jumped to his feet. "That was super helpful. You can leave now."

"I know his scent," she said hurriedly. "I was at Red's Bar the other night and overheard someone planning the attacks in the back. I don't know who it was, but his scent was familiar. I just can't place it. If I get near him again, I could tell you who it is."

Rosemary arched a brow. "You think we'd be willing to back you for that?"

"Let me help you figure it out." Kira bounced on her feet, her desperation bleeding through. "And once I sniff the guy out and you promise to back me, I'll tell you a few of the big players involved in the dark vampire project in Shadow Terrace."

Alex went so still I wasn't sure he was breathing, so I asked on his behalf, "How in the hell could you know about that?"

"I'm small, a fox, and I learned how to get around without notice." Kira lifted her chin. "I know a whole lot about this city, and I know how important finding out who is involved is to Alex, especially since you almost died multiple times because of them."

A loud banging sounded on the door past the elevator, then it burst open.

My heart raced as someone yelled, "Shadow City police!"

CHAPTER TWENTY

Ten police officers raced into the living room, followed by Ezra. The third wolf council member had the good sense to appear ashamed. His sea-green eyes looked everywhere but at Griffin and Sterlyn, and his normally olive skin seemed a tad pale.

"What the *hell* is going on?" Griffin spun toward him, nostrils flaring. "Why are you barging into my house?"

A man with caramel hair stepped forward beside Ezra and sneered. The hair was almost as thick on his arms and face as on the top of his head, and his biceps were larger than his head. "Because the council has ordered it."

Sterlyn stepped in front of Kira. "Why would they do that, Henry? And how the hell do you have a key to our condo?"

"The police have keys to every house in Shadow City, including members of the council," Griffin rasped.

Between that and the fact the city had police, every

bit of sense I thought I'd made of this world shifted, yet again, underneath me. I'd known they had guards, but I'd had no clue about actual police. Where had they been during the attack at the council building? Why had no one called them?

The other nine policemen stayed in the hallway, next to the resident elevator, unnerving me. It was as if they were waiting for a signal.

"And the front desk had to let us through without warning you." Ezra pulled at the collar of his mint-green polo shirt.

Alex tensed beside me. "Yes, but they're only to use the keys in an extreme emergency. They've never been used before now."

"There's nothing illegal going on here. And no one's hurt." Rosemary inched closer to me. "Why are you here?"

"Speaking of why someone is here." The smallest police officer, about my height, stepped to the front. Peeking out from under his black Shadow City police cap were wisps of ruby-colored hair. "What are you doing here, Kira? I'm sure your father will be interested."

Kira straightened her shoulders and glared at the man. "Why don't you mind your own business, Grady."

Grady. Her cousin.

"This is my business, seeing as you'll be reporting to me soon." Grady puffed out his chest as if to make himself more intimidating. "I'll repeat one more time. Why are you here?"

A few guys behind him snickered, putting Grady

more on edge. He had to be trying to prove something, not only to himself, but to his peers too.

"Now—" Kira started.

Sterlyn cut her off, her eyes cold. "The fact that you don't know why she's here speaks volumes about your strategy skills."

The tallest man behind Grady snorted. The caramel scruff on his face was longer than his slightly darker brown hair. His golden eyes reminded me of a lion. "Are you going to let a woman talk to you that way?"

"Shut up, Zach," Grady rasped.

"Sterlyn has a point, though." Henry grimaced as if that had been hard to admit. "Shifters attacked council members a few hours ago. Of course, they're pulling members of the community in for questioning."

Grady wrinkled his nose. "They were smart to start with a weak female who will spill everything...if she does know anything."

"At least, Kira was smart enough to figure things out." I had to be careful not to lie so they wouldn't realize Kira had come here of her own accord. "Without anyone having to explain it to her."

A grin slid into place on Kira's face.

Alex flinched. *Please don't draw attention to yourself. You're already on enough radars without siccing the police on us too.*

I should be quiet and let them continue hating on females? That infuriated me. *Nope. Maybe that's why the culture here isn't changing.* If I had to, I'd draw picket signs for every single female here. They deserved the same respect as the men, especially when the men's biceps were bigger than their brains.

That's not what I mean. Alex pinched the bridge of his nose and scooted closer to me. *I love you for sticking to your principles, but let me, Griffin, Sterlyn, or Rosemary do the talking until we get the whole forcing-you-to-turn situation dealt with. Please.*

"Look at what the council has resorted to." Henry stepped back. "Not only putting more females on the council but bringing in a human female who doesn't respect our hierarchy."

"There's no need for a pissing match." Rosemary stood, crossing her arms and turning to survey everyone in the room. "Apparently, you barged in for a reason. What is it?"

"Let me guess. You want to search Dad's old office?" Griffin leaned against the back of the couch. "You think there's something incriminating in there about the attack today."

Ezra straightened and ran his fingers through his sable hair, pushing it away from his face. "That's not why we're here." He seemed nervous but also resolved.

After a pause, Sterlyn cleared her throat. "Then why *are* you here?"

Henry and Ezra looked at me.

No. Why were they focusing on me?

Taking another step into the room, Ezra moved closer to Kira, and her eyes widened. She sniffed, and her face lined with concern.

"We're here for her," Ezra said.

As soon as those words had left his mouth, I didn't have to turn around to know I had the attention of every single cop in the room.

Kira took advantage of the distraction and mouthed, "That's him," to Alex and me.

Understanding washed over me, and my stomach dropped.

Ezra wouldn't do that to Griffin and Sterlyn. Despite him not saying much, he seemed to be on their side.

But maybe that was the point.

Perception was everything.

"Like hell you are," Alex hissed. His fangs descended, and he stood protectively in front of me. "She hasn't done a damn thing."

"Until the council makes its final decision," Ezra said as he shuffled toward us, "the girl will remain in custody so we can ensure she and the residents here stay safe."

Whoa. He had to be joking. "I'm not a threat to anyone. As you pointed out, I'm just a weak human *girl*."

"That may be the case," Henry snarled, "but five vampires died today because they couldn't resist your blood."

That was how they were spinning this. Because of me, vampires had died. That was true, but these people needed to learn to control their natural urges, especially if they planned on assimilating into the rest of the world, which, in my opinion, they desperately needed to do. They were so stuck in their ways that they needed to see the progress the rest of the world had made. It wasn't healthy to lock up an entire society, particularly when each race was trying to claw its way to the top.

"You're not taking her anywhere." Alex clenched his hands at his sides and glowered. "There are four council representatives right here, and an immediate decision can be made as long as there is a third there to approve it."

But if Kira meant what I feared, I had a feeling Ezra wouldn't side with us, and we would fall short of the third.

"I have spoken with Matthew, Erin, and Azbogah, and I agree with them." One corner of Ezra's mouth tipped upward, but he schooled his expression into a mask of indifference. "Unless there is *another* council member here."

"No." Griffin shook his head, and his eyes glowed. "You can't do this. I forbid it."

"Don't you dare try to alpha-will him." Henry stepped in front of Ezra. "Why do you think the police were called here and not the guard? The guard is mostly wolves, and the police force, though smaller, is made up of a mix of shifters. Your command won't work on. We were given the orders in case you tried to control Ezra and Reginald." He pointed to a man who was around six feet tall with a shaved head and tribal tattoos snaking over his arms.

"Do you seriously want to take on a silver wolf?" Sterlyn chuckled, and her skin glistened silver with her power.

"It's a new moon tonight." Ezra laughed. "You aren't stronger than anyone here."

"You won't get away with this." Rosemary flanked my other side, ready to protect me as well. "We won't allow you to take her."

I didn't want them to fight because of me. If I needed to go with them to ease the tension, I'd go voluntarily. I'd opened my mouth to say just that when chaos erupted.

Rosemary charged Ezra, her black wings exploding from her back.

As she approached him, Henry growled and lunged at the angel, crashing into her and taking them both to the floor.

"Get her!" Henry yelled.

Zach ran into the room, and Alex stood in front of me. Zach's golden eyes looked more animalistic as he charged toward me.

Blurring, Alex slammed into the cop, and they flew across the room and crashed into the glass. Somehow, the glass didn't shatter, reminding me that the materials here weren't from this world.

The other eight cops hurried toward me.

Griffin jumped over the couch and landed beside me. He stared at each one of them. "Do not touch her. You do not want to get on Sterlyn's bad side. Mine, either."

"You think we give a damn?" a guy who was half a foot shorter than Griffin asked. His head jerked to the side, reminding me of a bird, especially with the thin patch of stringy hair on top. "You won't be representing us much longer."

"Keep dreaming." Griffin spread his feet shoulder-width apart. "There's no way I'm handing over my position just because people keep coming at us."

The eight of them charged us, and Sterlyn cut off the back two, who were the lankiest of the bunch. She round kicked one in the face and punched the other in the jaw. They stumbled back as Zach and a tall, bronze man attacked Griffin.

Griffin threw his head back as Zach caught his arms and the rugged bronze man punched him in the stomach over and over again.

Crap, I had to help him. I jumped, but right before I could land on the rugged man, someone's arms wrapped around my stomach, catching me in midair.

"Did you really expect to help him?" my captor chuckled in my ear.

Yeah, I had, but I refused to humor him. Instead, I bucked, trying to get out of his hold.

No matter what I did, he didn't have a problem carrying me. He wrestled me past Sterlyn, who was fighting two other men. The first two were passed out on the floor.

Alex bulldozed Henry across the room and into the glass wall again. I watched in horror as Henry kicked Alex in the stomach and he bent over.

I needed to get to him. Going with my gut, I jerked my head back and smashed it into the face of the asshole holding me. With the amount of hair on his arms, I bet it was the other burly guy who'd stood near the back of the group.

A sharp pain filled my head, and the world spun. The asshole's chest shook with laughter.

"You can't hurt us," he rasped. "Supernaturals are way stronger than you could ever be."

Even if that were true, I wouldn't lie down without a fight. If I did whatever they wanted or expected from me, when would it ever end?

Mouth dry, I searched for the shadow, hoping it would come and help me, but I couldn't hold my head up, and vomit burned my throat. Where was the damn thing when I actually wanted it to show up? Could I summon it somehow?

"Take her," the guy holding me said. "She's about to pass out. I'll stay here and fight." He handed me off to an athletic man about Alex's height. His olive eyes locked on mine, and I immediately thought of a cat.

A loud hiss rang in my ears, and the hairy guy who'd been holding me grabbed Alex. Catching him hadn't been hard since Alex's attention was solely focused on me.

"Come on." Grady pushed through the living room toward us. "Let's get out of here."

"Like hell you will," Kira growled and tackled her cousin. Sneering, she wrapped her hands around his neck and squeezed. "I've been wanting to kick your ass for a long time."

"Go!" Ezra yelled. He dodged Rosemary's punch, but the angel didn't lose focus on her opponent.

The olive-eyed man threw me over his shoulder and raced for the door. He moved faster than I'd expected, and the world swirled even more. My only solace was the fact that my face wasn't right on his ass.

We sped past the residential elevator and crossed the short distance to the open door.

As the colorful lights from outside danced around me, I realized I'd never been out this way. He raced to an elevator in the hallway and pressed the down button.

The door didn't open immediately, buying time for someone to rescue me. I tried to gather myself. If I got on that elevator, the chances of Alex or someone else helping me would greatly diminish. I had to figure a way out of this myself.

I closed my eyes to center myself. My nausea worsened, but I kept them shut, hoping it would pass.

The elevator door dinged. I'd run out of time. As the door slid open, I did the only thing I knew to do. I opened my mouth wide and bit him right below his shoulder blade, silently praying it would be enough.

CHAPTER TWENTY-ONE

A pained grunt emanated from deep within his chest. He leaned over to throw me off his shoulder, but I kept my jaw tight and wrapped my arms around his waist, anchoring myself to him.

He reached around and grabbed a fistful of my hair.

My skull was on fire, but the pain cleared my dizziness, despite increasing my nausea. I tried to push through, but when he jerked, his shirt moved, loosening my hold. My teeth slammed together, and my neck popped, causing my ears to ring. I'd never felt as weak as I did now, which was saying something.

The guy forced me to the carpeted ground and rasped, "You're going to pay for that." His olive eyes glowed as he lifted his fist, and I closed my eyes.

I braced for impact, but his hovering presence disappeared, and then a scuffling sound followed.

Confused, I looked up to find Rosemary engaged in battle with the man. Her black wings lifted her as she flew around the cop, punching and kicking him continuously.

Thank God she'd gotten here because I had a feeling things had been about to get worse for me. I scanned the area since I'd never been in this hallway before. The walls were mostly concrete with small slits at the top to let light inside. The can lights in the ceiling likely turned on when it got dark.

I couldn't see any way out unless I took the elevator down or ran past Rosemary and the cop to go back inside the condo. Neither option was ideal. If I went down to the lobby, the cops would eventually follow. If I went back inside the condo, the fighting would continue.

What the hell should I do?

"Take that, you stupid jaguar." Rosemary punched the guy in the face.

The jaguar's eyes rolled back in his head as he crumpled.

She looked at me. "Go down to the lobby but stay indoors. We'll come down as soon as we can."

Okay, that made the decision easy. For once, I was glad someone had told me what to do.

I jumped into the elevator just as the doors started to close. Rosemary turned and flew back into the condo.

My heart hammered, and I took a deep breath. This elevator had no windows, but it felt luxurious with its wooden walls and muted gray carpet. Even though the space was at least six feet by six feet, after being manhandled, I felt claustrophobic.

Shadow City was massive, but the more time I spent

here, the smaller everything felt. I was ready to go back to Griffin and Sterlyn's comforting home in Shadow Ridge. Obviously, Alex and I needed to brainstorm our next steps, but I didn't want to broach that topic until the council had decided on my future.

Ugh. The thought turned my stomach. Being with Alex meant forfeiting my freedom of choice because, apparently, this council had the right to make important decisions for the supernatural races within their walls. The thought of Alex and me taking off from here and living our lives in Lexington with Annie and Eliza was becoming more and more attractive.

The number one flashed at the top of the elevator door. I wiped my sweaty palms on my jeans. All I had to do was find a place to hide and wait for Alex or my friends to retrieve me. I wouldn't consider the possibility that someone else would find me.

As the doors slid open, my world tilted.

Four men in the black Shadow City guard attire stood in front of me. The only other figure in the ginormous, all-glass lobby was a security person standing behind a dark cherrywood desk a few feet from the sliding glass door entrance.

I pressed the close-door button on the elevator, hoping it would magically close before one of them got to me, but alas, that didn't happen.

A man with roughly a foot on me in height grabbed my arm and pulled me from the elevator. He growled, "I knew those cops couldn't handle the job. They've never had to deal with worthy adversaries." The guy's gray eyes turned stormy.

"You told them, Wayne," said a guy with ash-blond hair so light it could be white. "But they didn't listen."

They were so strong and badass. I rolled my eyes internally. "Yeah, because it's not like Griffin and Sterlyn wouldn't've had you submitting to them within seconds of entering the room." Maybe angering them was a mistake.

"We weren't talking to you," the more muscular guy growled and stalked over to me. "Keep your mouth shut. Got it?"

Though he wasn't as big as Henry or the lion in the condo, he was close to the same size as Killian and looked just as strong.

"Do. You. Understand?" he asked slowly.

He'd told me to keep my mouth shut, so what was a girl to do? I nodded while lifting the middle finger of my free hand at him. I grinned maliciously, wanting him to know I wasn't complying but rather being a complete and utter smartass.

His chest heaved. "You—"

"Cody, chill," a man with salt-and-pepper hair barked. "She didn't say a word like you asked. It's not her fault you weren't smart enough to include gestures as well."

"Da-ad..." Cody complained.

This was a fun and interesting family dynamic. Now that the older man had caught my attention, I could tell he and Cody were related. They had the same starry-blue eyes and were about the same height. Besides the age and hair, the other main difference was that the older man wasn't as thick as his son.

"That's enough." The older man gestured to a black Suburban parked outside the building. "Let's get her in the car before the alpha and alpha mate come down."

Okay, he was smarter than the other three. That didn't sit well with me.

My arm tingled from Wayne's grip. I was going to have bruises where his fingers dug into my skin. I connected with Alex. *Please tell me you're on your way down to the lobby.* I glanced over my shoulder to find that the number one was still glowing, indicating that the elevator hadn't moved.

I should've hit the top floor button before Wayne dragged me out.

We're practically done up here, Alex responded. *Just stay out of sight.*

Easier said than done. I searched for a weapon, but the room was bare except for the desk, and I wasn't strong enough to lift it and throw it at them. If I made it out of this in one piece, I'd get a dagger like Sterlyn's and keep it strapped to me. Now I understood why she always carried it.

Concern wafted through our connection. *What do you mean?*

Four guards were waiting for me in front of the elevator. They snatched me before the doors could close, and they have a Suburban outside to take me somewhere.

Dammit. Alex's anger was suffocating. *I'm going to*

fight my way out and head to you now. Do whatever you can to stay put.

That helped tremendously.

"We've got to go." Salt and Pepper headed toward the door.

"You heard him," Wayne rasped and jerked me forward. His grip tightened as if he expected me to fight him.

I needed to throw him off. I flinched and stuck out my bottom lip in a pout. "Okay. Please stop hurting me," I whimpered. I hated pretending to be weak, but if I wanted to get away, I'd have to play into their perceptions of humans.

"Oh, gods," Cody groaned. "I get she's that vampire prince's mate, but how can he deal with this?"

Ash Blond shook his head. "None of us have found our mates, so it's not like we can understand. Maybe it's endearing to him?"

"Really?" Cody wrinkled his nose in disgust. "You're taking up for a fucking vampire?"

I wanted to ask if they liked anyone besides the wolves, but I bit my tongue. That would interfere with my plan.

"No," Ash Blond sneered. "I'm saying the royal vampire family is ruthless. He wouldn't put up with anything that grated on his nerves."

"You should be careful. It sounds like you respect bloodsuckers," Wayne warned, dragging me toward the door. "People might think you're turning soft."

"Shut it," Salt and Pepper snapped and spun around

to look at us. "The council members should be respected. You know what could happen if anyone overheard you speaking against a member."

Luckily, Wayne was either distracted or falling for my weak routine because his grip on my arm softened. Tiny prickles filtered through my skin as circulation returned to my arm. If I ran now, they'd catch me in seconds.

Walking as slowly as possible, I glanced over my shoulder. The elevator had begun moving upward. *Please tell me you called the elevator.*

Yes. Alex sounded anxious. *And Rosemary is on her way down too.*

Thank God.

As I stepped outside, Salt and Pepper opened the trunk of the Suburban. He waved for the three of them to hurry up.

I moaned, pretending I was in pain, hoping Wayne would loosen his grip more. I could yank out of his hold, but it would hurt like hell. If he'd loosen it a smidgen more, getting away would be easier.

The colors wove around me in time with my heartbeat. As far as I could see, only us five were out here, so I didn't have to worry about a vampire attacking me.

At the door to the Suburban, I inhaled, ready to make my move. I longed to glance skyward to see if Rosemary was close by, but I didn't want to alert the guards.

I had to bank on her super speed.

Alex connected with me. *I'll be down in a minute. I'm out the front door of the condo.*

Okay. Easy-peasy. I could totally stall. I lowered my head as if to enter the Suburban. Then I pivoted on my heel and jerked as hard as possible out of Wayne's hold.

His hand dropped, releasing me completely.

Maybe, for once, fate was on our side. I'd taken two running steps toward the foyer when thick arms wrapped around me and squeezed me so hard that all the air whooshed out of my lungs.

I tried to breathe, but the hold was so tight that my lungs couldn't refill.

"Get her in there now!" Ash Blond yelled. "The angel is here!"

My head spun from lack of oxygen. The corners of my vision darkened as my body was propelled forward. I hit the cement, and my face, arms, and legs burned. Whoever caught me had landed on top of me, and I'd hit the ground harder than normal.

When I'd thought I couldn't breathe earlier, I'd been so wrong. Under the weight of this man, my body screamed for air while heat licked all over my body.

The squealing of a vehicle pulling up echoed in my ears. I hoped like hell the guards didn't have backup.

The man rolled off me, and I turned my head, sucking in the deepest breath I'd ever taken. Before I could do much more than that, arms lifted me up, and I found myself staring at Cody's face. He grimaced and threw me into the car.

Something warm dripped down my cheek and onto my shirt. I looked down. A stream of blood trickled onto the fabric.

Shit.

I glanced at my arms and legs. My shirt and jeans were torn, blood seeping through. No wonder I was in so much damn pain. I'd hate to see my face.

Black wings flashed by the car window, and Rosemary tackled Wayne. Cody fought dirty by punching her in the kidneys.

The doors of the Suburban behind us flung open, and cops poured from the vehicle with guns.

Shit. Things were getting out of hand.

Rosemary cried in rage and took flight upward, disentangling herself from Cody. I'd never heard her sound that angry before.

She wrapped her wings around her and began to spin, faster and faster, until she blurred into a dark cylinder of fury.

"We gotta get out of here!" Salt and Pepper yelled. He lunged inside the car next to me and slammed the door shut.

The front passenger door opened, and Cody climbed in. Another guard was already in the driver's seat.

"Go!" Salt and Pepper demanded.

"But—" The driver gestured at Ash Blond and Wayne.

Salt and Pepper smacked the back of his headrest. "Go. Now. They'll be fine, once we're out of here."

With shaking hands, I lunged to open my door. Salt and Pepper dove over me and clamped his hands on my wrists. He yanked me away from the door to face him.

Frantic, I twisted my head around to see where Rosemary was.

The driver threw the car into gear at the same time the front door to the building flew open. Alex's eyes widened in horror as he watched us pull away.

CHAPTER TWENTY-TWO

"Drive faster," Salt and Pepper yelled, and the Suburban lurched forward, wheels squealing. Gunshots were fired as the car sped off. "The cops are engaging so we can get away."

We barreled down the road at seventy miles per hour, and I stared out the back window as long as I could. Another vehicle appeared as the building disappeared behind us with Rosemary still engaged in battle.

I could only hope and pray that Alex and Rosemary didn't become injured in the gunfire.

Anger wafted through our connection as Alex used it to communicate with me. *Veronica, do not worry. We will get you out of there, but whatever you do, don't let them know we can communicate like this, especially since it's intermittent.*

Don't they know? They knew we were mates. Wouldn't they assume we could connect mentally?

No, not since you're human. I told Gwen not to tell

anyone. Add in the fact that our connection is rather hit or miss, and we've been able to stay under the radar. Matthew thinks we found you in the blood bank because of Sterlyn and the wolves since everyone watched them sniff out that hidden door.

Okay, so we had one advantage. I'd take it. *Just stay safe so you can get me the hell out of wherever they're taking me.*

I love you, and I'll be careful. They don't want to hurt us unless they absolutely have to. They're holding us off from chasing you. Alex pushed his emotions toward me. *Be safe. Please.*

Back at you. I couldn't actually form the words back to him without crying. My throat dried up, and between this and all the pain I was in, if I started to cry, I wasn't sure if I could stop. I latched on to the love he pushed toward me, needing it more than anything.

That was what it took for me to decide.

Forever wasn't long enough with him, and if I stayed human, we'd have to continue fighting, not only our enemies, but everyone too. The best way for us to be together and happy was for me to turn. Maybe it wasn't ideal, but when had my life ever been picture perfect? And maybe, if I learned how to control my urges, Eliza and Annie could still be part of my life. If I never aged, it would raise questions, but we could figure that out as we went.

It was clear that Alex and the wolves were truly friends. Turning wouldn't negate my relationship with them. I knew that now. It had taken this disaster of a show, though, for me to understand that.

All my uncertainty fell by the wayside. This was the right choice for me, and thankfully, it was mine and not forced on me by the council. They might think I was bowing to their whims, but I didn't give a shit. Maybe it would get them off our backs.

Growing up in the system, I'd learned that if a warden thought they'd forced my hand, even when they hadn't, my life became easier. Who cared what the council thought if I knew the truth?

Strength coursed through me, overriding the hysteria that had been creeping in. If I wanted Alex to turn me on our own time, I needed to use my head and get out of this situation.

"Where are you taking me?" Though I felt strong, my voice quivered from the overwhelming emotions that were still subsiding.

Good. That made me sound weak and scared.

"A maximum-security location," Salt and Pepper answered, not bothering to slacken his hold.

My stomach dropped, and I couldn't hide my worry. "Where you keep dangerous supernaturals? What about the vampires there?" When Matthew had captured Eilam, I'd learned that one form of punishment for vampires was starvation. Bringing in a human seemed like a terrible idea.

Salt and Pepper's voice softened as his face smoothed. "We know we can't keep you around starving vampires. There are only shifters where we're taking you."

Hope blossomed in my stomach. "Wolves?" Griffin and Sterlyn could command the wolves to let them in.

"Oh, no." Cody laughed. "The council is smarter than that. Other types of shifters will guard you, and once you're inside, you'll be well protected, just like all the old artifacts, where no one can get to you. And we waited outside so Griffin wouldn't know about our involvement and force us to bring you back."

That sounded like a threat. It also sounded like Alex would know exactly where they were taking me. I'd tell him next time we connected.

"Shut up," Salt and Pepper snapped. "We want to reassure her, not tell her everything."

I had to give it to him for not being completely stupid, but I was grateful his son was.

Alex? I was still distraught, so I should be able to connect.

His concern slammed into me. *Yes. Are you hurt?*

No. I hated that I'd made him worry, but I didn't have much of a choice. *Tell Griffin that wolves have me. Cody and his dad. Maybe he can alpha-will them to bring me back.*

Hope replaced his worry. *I didn't realize they were wolves. Let me break away and get upstairs to Griffin.*

As if reading my mind, my captor reached behind our seats and pulled out a sack. Turning to me, he gazed at my face and winced. "I'm sorry, but we have to put this on you. If you promise not to fight me, I'll release you so it's as painless as possible."

What the hell was on the sack, powder that would burn my skin?

Afraid to ask, I nodded.

Something passed through his eyes. "Lock the doors, and Cody, if she even looks like she's thinking about escaping, stop her."

"Ha ha." Cody sneered. "If she tries anything, I'll sack her too."

His dad frowned.

"Get it?" Cody gestured at the bag in his father's hand. "You're going to sack her while I might need to sack her."

"Son, I got it." Salt and Pepper shook his head. "I just don't find it funny."

Cody's face fell.

Good. The guy was an asshole. I bet if he thought he had a chance of taking over the council, he'd try it in a heartbeat. Hell, apparently, every supernatural wanted to be at the top and were waiting for the right opportunity to make a play.

Like Ezra.

The bastard.

Salt and Pepper released my arm and turned to me. He spread open the bag and lifted it over my head, then slowly lowered it over my face.

That was when I realized what he'd meant by hurting me. The side of my face that was raw from hitting the ground burned as the cloth brushed against it. Though the material was smooth, it might as well have been sand-paper. I tried to remain still, but as he tied the bag at my throat, I jerked away. If it hurt this bad sliding on, I didn't want to consider how it would feel when they removed it. A shudder racked my body.

"There," Salt and Pepper rasped. "Done."

Even without a supernatural nose, the metallic stench of my blood nearly made me retch. They hadn't cut holes in the bag, so I was breathing the same air over and over.

Babe, what's wrong? Alex connected with so much angst that my heart cracked. *Are they hurting you? You're in pain.*

Well, obviously I was in pain if he had to ask. *Salt and Pepper wasn't trying to hurt me. He put a bag over my head so I can't see where we're going.*

Salt and Pepper? he asked. *And dammit, you have no clue where you're going.*

Actually, I might. Cody said something about it. I repeated the description.

They're taking you to the artifact building. That complicates things. I'm in the elevator, heading back up to the condo to let Griffin know.

They said it would be safer and harder for anyone to get to me. Even though I didn't know why.

He sighed. *We can get into the foyer, but I bet they've already restricted us from being able to go farther. The building is protected by guards and magic.*

Great. The news kept getting better.

Rosemary's trying to reach you.

She could fly faster than Alex could run, so maybe she could get to me in time. Just as I thought that, the Suburban slowed, and my heart stopped. *I think we're here.*

How? Surprise pulsed through the bond. *It's across the city.*

This I could answer. *They drove fast.*

His rage almost suffocated me, especially since I had the damn bag over my head. The vehicle turned off, confirming I was right.

"I'm removing the bag," Salt and Pepper warned, and he lifted the bottom. My cuts must have dried because, as he raised the material, it felt like he was removing skin from my face.

I whimpered, unable to hold the sound in, and my chest heaved as he jerked it away from my face.

Veronica! Worry had replaced Alex's anger. *What's wrong?*

They removed the bag. I'm skinned up from falling outside the condo, and the bag stuck to my cheek. I couldn't see much through my tears, but the light was dim. *I think we're already in the building.*

You're injured? That's why I keep feeling your pain. What happened?

I tried to get away, and Cody tackled me. The more I thought about it, the worse everything hurt. *I hit the ground with his entire weight on me. My leg, arm, and half my face are pretty messed up.*

They're going to pay, he promised.

I blinked the tears from my eyes. Dwelling on things I

couldn't change wouldn't get us anywhere. I had to concentrate on the present.

After a few seconds, my vision cleared, and I looked around. *We're in a warehouse. There are tons of boxes. Does that sound right?*

There is a garage for special deliveries. They must have suspected that Rosemary or I would follow, and they took you in that way. Bastards. I think this is the first time a person has been the delivery.

Salt and Pepper opened his door and climbed out. He gestured for me to follow.

Part of me wanted to cross my arms and refuse to move, but that wouldn't bode well for me. I needed to play along until I could figure a way out of this situation, or until Alex and the others found me.

There had to be something I could do.

Taking a deep breath, I pushed the pain away. Cody and the driver flanked Salt and Pepper, waiting for me to climb out.

I took my time and scoped out the garage. The loading door was already closed. Inching toward the three guards, I gently touched my face and forced myself to wince, hoping to appear weak. I pulled my hand away, and my fingertips came away wet with blood. I grimaced. Maybe it wasn't only an impression. Despite the whole bag situation, at least, my wound hadn't reopened completely.

Cody snagged my arm and dragged me the rest of the way out.

"Son," Salt and Pepper growled. "Do *not* manhandle her."

"Oh, stop." Cody brushed him off, but he stopped tugging so hard. "She's just a human."

"Of which we are half," his dad snapped. "Our humanity molds us as much as our animal, and we need to respect both sides. You forgetting that puts you on par with vampires, who lose their humanity, and even some of the angels."

His frankness surprised me. It sounded like something Sterlyn would say. If that was how he felt, why was he opposing his alpha?

The three of them grabbed their heads.

Yes! Griffin was using his alpha will on them.

"I'm so sorry," the older man rasped, then did what he'd just scolded his son for and dragged me across the garage toward an inner door.

Sweat sprouted above his lip as if he were fighting something. He pounded on the thick wooden door and yelled, "Get her now!"

He crumpled to the floor, and I jerked from his grasp. I spun to find all three of them on the ground, groaning in terrible pain.

Before they could regain their composure, I searched the driver's pocket and grabbed the car keys. He tried to grasp my hand, but he groaned and clutched his head again as Griffin continued the assault.

Keys in hand, I pivoted on my heels and raced toward the garage door. There had to be a button to open it.

I pushed myself harder than ever before. My legs and

arms flamed from my injuries, but I ignored the sting. When I reached the door, I searched the walls and started pressing random buttons, but nothing worked.

They'd opened the door from the Suburban some-how. Maybe they had a garage door opener. I ran for the vehicle. Three men charged through the door that Salt and Pepper had knocked on.

"Get them out of here," the tallest one commanded. "I'll get the girl."

I had no time to waste.

CHAPTER TWENTY-THREE

The tallest one had a physique similar to the panther, with the same dark olive skin. I was shit out of luck since he could probably run just as fast, but I refused to not even try.

Giving up had never been an option, and I wouldn't let it be one now.

As expected, every foot I moved forward, he gained at least five on me. But it didn't matter. My goal was to get to the vehicle and reverse, destroying the garage door if I had to.

The guy might be fast, but he wasn't invincible. I'd bet a Suburban could kick his ass.

I focused on moving forward and not glancing over my shoulder as adrenaline pumped through my body.

I welcomed it.

My pain receded, and my head cleared, the fight or flight response taking hold. Somehow, I was moving at a blurring speed, and I wouldn't analyze why.

When I reached the bumper, I almost pumped my arm in victory. Maybe I would get out of here. The thought reinvigorated me, and I realized why leaders said hope was dangerous. It made impossible situations seem less intimidating.

I grasped the door handle to the driver's side as my attacker rounded the bumper.

Ugh, I'd gotten too cocky. As my hand jerked back and the door opened, the man grabbed my waist and pulled me away. Cat-like lime-green eyes stared at me, confirming my jaguar hypothesis, and he said gently, "Please, don't fight us." He scanned my face and frowned. "It looks like you're injured enough. I promise nothing more will happen if you cooperate." He shut the door and released his hold, towering over me.

Yeah, if I tried to run, he'd get me. That was why he wasn't concerned. I might have been running fast for me but definitely not for him. I lifted my chin, channeling as much defiance as possible. "And if I don't cooperate?"

"I'll have to escort you against your will, but I'd rather it not come to that." He sighed and ran a hand through his shaggy, toffee-colored hair. "You're a vampire princess, by all rights. We don't want to upset Alex."

I laughed way too loudly, the sound bordering on insanity even to my ears. "You think he's not *upset*?"

"Fair point, but our goal was never to rough you up." He exhaled. "We weren't there to oversee taking you into custody. You will be treated fairly and respectfully, but you have to remain here."

"But I don't want to." I had nothing to lose. This

entire situation was crap. "And Alex, Griffin, and Sterlyn are upset that you arrested me."

He lifted his hands in surrender. "It wasn't an arrest."

I wanted whatever he was smoking. "Cops showed up at the door and took me against my will."

He nodded slowly. "But it wasn't to take you to jail. It was to bring you somewhere safe, for you and for others. This wasn't meant to happen."

"You expected cops and guards to show up and force me to come with them and thought a fight *wouldn't* happen?" I had to say it out loud for him to realize how stupid that sounded.

He laughed but didn't smile. "I realize how that sounds, and I warned Ezra it wouldn't go well, but he didn't care."

Kira's distrust had been confirmed. She'd been honest earlier, and now we knew who the traitor was. That counted for something. "But he's just one of the shifter representatives." We both knew that, but I wanted to see his reaction.

"Others also ordered me, so my hands are tied." He held out a hand to me. "Can we please be amicable for all our sakes?"

When he put it like that, my perspective changed. Even though fighting the council's decision hadn't been smart, I hadn't realized how bad it was. Maybe if Ezra had talked to us like this, instead of barging in and abducting me, things would've gone better. Hell, they could've let Alex come with me. That would have made things exponentially better.

But Ezra had wanted this to happen.

And we'd fallen into the trap.

The best thing I could do was be reasonable. "Fine." I shook his hand. "But don't make me regret this."

"I'm Roman." He shook my hand back. "And I won't. We truly are just supposed to keep you here—and safe—until the next meeting."

"In two days?" Being stuck somewhere against my will for two days didn't sound like fun, but if it helped Alex and the others, I'd stay put.

He didn't respond, remaining stoic.

Yeah, I wouldn't have been thrilled about answering that either if I were him, but he was being nice, so I'd be civil. "I'm Veronica."

A kind smile inched across his face. "I know. Come on, let's get you settled."

The urge to jump in the car overwhelmed me, but Roman was only three feet away. I wouldn't make it in before he captured me. I needed to go back to my original plan: be complacent until I saw another opportunity. At least, this guy seemed nice, like Salt and Pepper, and he was only doing his job.

Pushing away the urge to flee, I allowed Roman to escort me toward the door. The two men from earlier and the wolves were gone. I hadn't even heard a scuffle. "Are they okay?" I shouldn't care, but only Cody had been an asshole.

"They had to be ushered out. Griffin used his alpha will on them." Roman pursed his lips. "He must have been notified that they'd taken you and made the call. Six months ago, I never thought I'd be saying that in the same sentence as his name."

That was an odd thing to say. "What do you mean?" Griffin was strong, especially with Sterlyn by his side. The two of them could take on the world and win. Okay, maybe that was an exaggeration, but raw power emanated from them, and I would never want to go up against them.

I looked around at the racks of boxes. I found it odd that rare artifacts would be left so close to an outside door.

"Before the silver wolf surfaced, he was floundering and not wanting to lead." Roman opened the door and waved his hand. "A lot happened in the two years after his father's death, and when he finally stepped into power, it made many who were aligned with Dick unhappy. The silver wolf makes things worse."

Why in the world was he telling me all of this? I wanted to ask but held my tongue. I didn't want him to stop talking. Instead, I'd act stupid and hope he leaked more information. "Dick?"

I stepped through the door and into a long hallway that reminded me of every warehouse in the human world. The lighting wasn't great, but I doubted it hindered the jaguar. The beige walls inched toward me. My shoes squeaked against the tile floor; I wouldn't be able to sneak away without alerting them.

"His father's beta. Griffin asked him to lead in his stead. Dick formed many alliances within the shifter realm and elsewhere." Roman pointed down the hallway, staying beside me. "We're going to follow the hallway until we're forced to turn right."

Obeying, I moved slowly, trying to stop my shoes from squeaking, but no matter my speed, they gave away my presence. Light on his feet, Roman didn't make a sound. "I've never made so much noise walking before."

"Oh, that." He chuckled warmly. "That's a spell. It's one way to catch intruders."

"Will my shoes be spelled to stop making so much noise?" I wanted to learn everything magic could do.

"No, I'm sorry." He stayed close behind me. "But your room is safe. We got Erin to undo the floor spell in there for you since you'll be spending most of your time there."

I bet that witch had loved every minute of prepping the room for me. The woman was breathtaking, but her maliciousness consumed her.

Not sure what else to say and not wanting to pry so much that he'd shut down, I remained silent, squeaking my way to my prison cell.

As instructed, I turned down another long hallway with four doors on the right and three on the left.

"You're the first door on the left," he said. "But do you need to use the bathroom first?"

"Actually, yes, I'd like to clean up a little." I looked at my arm and leg. "Wash up so I don't get an infection or something."

He scratched his head. "It's the second door on the right."

Wanting to be alone, I hurried to the door and threw

it open. I turned to close it, only to find Roman leaning against the wall across from me.

I guessed I should've been happy that he hadn't demanded to come in with me. I flicked on the lights to find a three-stall bathroom. I didn't know why, but I'd expected it to be a one-stall place.

They must have had more people working here than I'd considered.

I headed to the farthest sink on the left and peered in the mirror—and regretted it. My face looked worse than my arms and legs. I'd almost say it had been put through a meat grinder. I wasn't getting out of this without scarring. No wonder the bag had felt like sandpaper.

Blood crusted the skin, and if I smiled too wide, the wound cracked open. I regretted coming in here. Pain flared through my body, stealing my breath. I needed comfort, and since my emotions were still heightened, I reached out to the one person who made the world seem right. *Are you there?*

Always, Alex connected back. *Did they do something to you?*

No. I grabbed some paper towels and turned on the water to warm. *I...I just feel so alone.* I'd never felt this broken before, not even as a child. Finding Alex had given me so many things, and the realization of what I could lose made me feel insane.

Hey, we will get you, he vowed. *We're working on calling an emergency hearing with the council. They can't take one of our own like that.*

We both knew it was futile. *They'll say they had at*

least a third in agreement and it was an emergency due to the shifter attack.

But they can't make that call. Alex's positivity comforted me. *We decided as a council that you would stay at Sterlyn and Griffin's until your fate was determined. They can't strip that away without a full council meeting.*

Thank God. I hoped that was true because I'd been worried I would be stuck here for the next two days without him. I lathered my stinging hands. *Won't they decide on my fate sooner because of that?*

No. I think we can put off their decision since there's so much turmoil with the shifters.

I couldn't think of any reason to put it off. *I don't want them to decide on my behalf. I have made my decision.* I was glad we weren't together for this conversation. Depending on his reaction, it might be too hard to see his face. Either way, it wouldn't matter.

Babe, it's okay. He pushed reassurance toward me. *I would never force you to become a vampire. Being a human is the best way to ensure your soul stays pure.*

Maybe when I'd first learned of this world, I'd have agreed.

But not now.

No, the type of person you want to be defines who you are. I needed him to understand, and once I laid everything on the table, he wouldn't fight me. *You're a vampire, and you never lost your humanity.*

But it's a struggle, and believe me, people have tempted me. His disgust flowed through me. *It's been easier since you've arrived, but I never want you to experience that.*

Even with the temptation, you persevered. He had to see himself through my eyes. *Even when you didn't have me, you still were this person. You wouldn't have become friends with Sterlyn, Griffin, and Rosemary if that person wasn't you.*

He paused for a second. *What are you saying?*

Even forever wouldn't be long enough beside you. God, I sounded cheesy, but I meant every word. I wanted him to understand that I had no doubts. *And I want to turn. After seeing you fight alongside our friends and realizing there's always a chance that I'll never see you again, I know I want to always be by your side, for as long as you want me.*

Are you sure? he asked tentatively.

A smile spread until my face hurt. *Yes, and I want you to turn me.*

Happiness flowed into me, and I wished I'd waited to tell him in person. I'd been afraid he'd try to talk me out of it; I hadn't expected him to like what he heard.

Are you sure? The happiness tamped down. *I don't want you to feel pressured.*

I don't. If anything, it was the opposite. *I came to this decision all on my own.*

You don't know how happy that makes me. You mean more to me than anything, and I want to do everything possible to make you happy. I love you so damn much that it's hard to breathe sometimes, and there is nothing I want more than to have you by my side for eternity. You aren't alone and never will be, whether you stay human or turn.

His words warmed my heart, and I wanted to kiss him and seal our promise.

And of course, I'll turn you. I'd kill anyone before they could get that close to you.

The ache of loneliness eased, and I quickly cleaned my face, arm, and leg. Even though we didn't say anything more, I could feel his joy wafting between us.

I gently patted the ugly scrapes dry. My face hadn't improved, but at least it was clean. I headed back out into the hallway to find Roman still standing there.

He smiled at me as he examined me. "Better?"

"Nope, but clean." I couldn't get upset because Alex and I had figured out our future—somewhat. It was the most we'd ever decided before.

He escorted me to my door, and I entered a room that looked identical to the hallway, except with cheap brown carpet instead of tile. A small desk with a wooden chair sat in the corner with a clock hanging above it. There was a bookshelf with a few titles on the shelves, and a small cot with white sheets and a thin beige blanket nearby. A commercial-sized air vent in the center of the ceiling blew cool air over us, making me chill. I was thankful for the sheet on the cot that I could use to cover up.

"Sorry, we had to convert an office into a room for you, but the cot is comfortable. I've used it a few times." He frowned. "I'll bring you dinner in a couple of hours. Do you need anything between then and now?"

I shook my head, ready to be alone. A book on the

shelf, titled *Broken Mate,* caught my eye. "No, I'm good. Thank you."

He nodded. "Just yell if you need anything." He walked out the door, and I heard the click behind him. Reality sank in. I was a prisoner here, but at least he was nice. The situation could have been way worse.

My eyes grew heavy, and I climbed onto the cot, ignoring the fact that others had slept on it. It was no different from staying in a hotel, but at least, at a hotel, you had a private bathroom and could come and go as you pleased.

Roman had been right, and the cot was quite comfortable. I'd drifted off to sleep before I even realized it.

CONCERN WAFTED THROUGH ME, and my eyes popped open. I glanced around, disoriented, until the beige walls and desk reminded me. How long had I slept? The clock said six, but it could have been evening or early morning. No food had been left for me, so my gut said evening.

Veronica, Alex connected to me. *We've got a huge problem. My brother is on his way to you.*

CHAPTER TWENTY-FOUR

My body tightened as the words sank in. Why the hell would Matthew come here? I didn't trust him, and for him to seek me out without Alex threw up a huge red flag. *I...I don't know what to do.* Fear trickled through me, seizing my chest. I hated that the bastard had such an impact on me, but he was similar to many of the foster parents I'd grown up with—manipulative and selfish, though he loved to give the illusion that he was a saint.

We're on our way. Alex's anger picked up a notch. *You don't need to worry.*

He could feel my fear and was trying to calm me, but we knew he couldn't promise that.

The air turned off, forcing my attention to the vent. It was an industrial-size vent, and a plan sprang into my mind. *I might have a way out.* It might be crazy, but hell, I didn't have much to lose, especially if Matthew was coming.

Alex's trepidation surged between us. *What are you talking about?*

I had to be confident. *I'm going to climb into the air shaft through the vent. I can travel outward and drop into the lobby.*

That's a horrible idea, Alex connected. *Just stay put. I'll be there soon.*

They wouldn't let him in. The blasted door was shut, and the room had no windows, so I couldn't see into the hallway, but I placed my ear to the door and held my breath.

I didn't hear anything. Roman would be bringing my dinner soon, so I needed to go. Maybe they'd hold off on bringing me food before the vampire king's arrival, assuming they knew he was coming.

I inched the desk underneath the air vent. The cover was the same size as a ceiling tile, so I could move it to the side and get through.

Once I'd positioned the desk, I remained quiet and listened. Silence greeted me again.

Moving slowly and steadily, I climbed onto the desk and squatted. I waited a moment, ensuring it could hold my weight. When the desk remained stable, I stood and exhaled with relief.

My fingers reached the vent, and I stood on my tiptoes and pushed the cover upward and to the left. I forced myself not to move too quickly so I wouldn't make more noise than necessary. As I slid the vent onto the backside of a ceiling tile, a low screech had me holding my breath. With shifter hearing, that might as well have been a siren.

Hoping that the shifters were far away enough not to hear anything, I tried pulling myself up, but I couldn't. Dammit, I had to do something.

As if I'd called it, the shadow appeared beside me.

I snorted without humor. "Really? You couldn't show up earlier so I wouldn't be in this situation?"

The shadow shook its head like it didn't like my attitude.

Go figure.

But at least it was here now.

Its arms separated from its body and wrapped around me. Cold bit through my shirt, but I didn't budge since it was trying to help me. It lifted me up, helping me climb into the vent.

As soon as I got inside, I stilled, hoping no one had heard anything. If they had, they'd rush in here any second, and if I was hanging out over the room, I'd have no chance to escape.

I dragged myself into the square duct and tried to prevent my elbows from banging into the metal, but it was no use. Even breathing made a squeak. Dammit, I hadn't thought this through.

I glanced around, expecting the shadow to be there to help me again, but I was alone. For the first time ever, I missed the pesky thing.

I could do nothing but move forward. The clanging from my movements hurt my ears, and I prayed it wasn't as loud as I feared.

In too deep to stop, I dragged my body over the metal while tears pooled in my eyes from the pain. I'd planned to put the air vent cover back in place, but they'd be able to smell what I'd done, and the desk gave away my location.

Desperate, I tried clamping down on the pain and stress, but apparently, I didn't handle it well.

Is Matthew there? Alex connected, anger lapping over me. *We're five minutes out. I'll kill the bastard.*

No, he's not. I couldn't allow Alex to come here, ready to declare war, when my turmoil was because I'd followed through on my stupid plan. I tried moving slowly, but it didn't eliminate the noise. This was not how it worked in movies. People were able to get out this way without alerting anyone to their presence.

Then what's—? He cut off. Then his anger was replaced with reluctant amusement. *For the love of the gods, please tell me you didn't go into the air vent.*

Yeah, it hadn't been my greatest plan. *I was desperate.*

Instead of an answer, all I felt was fear, pride, and disbelief.

All well-deserved. Well, the fear and disbelief, anyway. I continued to inch through the vent, wanting to at least get into a different room. That should buy me a few more minutes. My heart pounded as I waited to hear footsteps, screams, or people talking. They'd be here any second.

I reached the vent of the next room and figured I'd better cut my losses while I still could. Something *yanked* at me, but I ignored the feeling as I stuck my fingers through the air vent's slits and jerked upward. The metal groaned, but it lifted, and I pushed it aside.

"Do you hear that?" Roman said from nearby. "We need to check on the girl."

Before I could overthink it, I slipped through the hole and dropped to my feet. I landed hard on the floor in a very dim room. The only light filtered in through the cracks around the door that led to the hallway.

Footsteps pounded toward me, and terror swarmed through me. Maybe I should've stayed put, but I didn't want to wait around for Matthew to decide my fate all on his own. As a foster kid, I'd often see the wardens ask for forgiveness rather than permission, and I wouldn't be surprised if he came here planning to turn me himself.

My gut told me that was his plan, so I had to stall until Alex and the others got here. *Please tell me you're here.*

We're pulling up. If you hear Matthew's voice, just know I'm right behind him.

Yeah, that didn't bring me much comfort, seeing as they would let Matthew in and not Alex.

Something brushed my hand. I couldn't make out anything at first. Then faintly glowing green eyes materialized in front of me, and the shadow took form. I jerked away out of instinct, but the shadow's grip tightened, and I relaxed.

The men were right outside my room, and I heard the door open. I wanted to be quiet, but the shadow dragged me across the room.

Why did this thing keep showing up? What did it want? Every time I forgot to worry about it, the shadow reared its ugly face. Well, okay. Not its face but its presence.

"Distract the vampire king while I look for her," Roman commanded. "She couldn't have gotten far."

"Are you sure?" a man asked.

"Just go," Roman growled.

My feet hit something hard, causing a loud bang. I gritted my teeth to stop myself from crying out, but the pain was so intense that I fell to the floor.

The men went quiet, and then Roman said in shock, "She's in the hidden-artifact collection."

As the men reached the door I was hiding behind, the cool hand grabbed my wrist and guided it upward to pull out a box from the shelf above me. I tried to free my wrist, but the *yank*ing I'd felt in the vent took hold. As if my body had a mind of its own, my hand found the edges of the box, opened it, and reached inside.

At first, I didn't feel anything. Then my hand brushed something sharp, piercing my skin. A key slid into the door lock.

I jerked my hand away, but my blood heated inside me. I stumbled back and fell on my ass. Warmth spread through my body.

The door flew open, letting light flood in, and Roman stepped inside. His eyes narrowed on me. "What are you doing?" he asked. "This room is secured. How did you get in?"

As I opened my mouth to say something...anything...

my blood began to boil. I whimpered and yanked my fingers through my hair, pulling at the roots. I wanted another sensation to focus on, but it didn't matter. I couldn't feel the pain of pulling my hair.

Roman kneeled beside me, his face lined with concern. "Veronica, what's wrong?"

I wanted to answer him, but I couldn't. Agony ripped through me. My blood burned so hot that my skin felt as if it were melting. *Alex, I need you.* If I was dying, I needed to be with him one more time. I could die gazing at the man I loved.

"Something's wrong," Alex said clearly as if he were right beside me.

Turning my head, I expected to see him at the door, but he was nowhere. Was I imagining him?

Tears blurred my vision, and I withered.

"Stop being dramatic," Matthew scoffed. "You can't see her. Only I'm allowed to see her."

Roman touched my arm. "We need to get you back to your room before he comes back."

A scream coursed through me, but I wasn't sure if I'd yelled internally or not. I wanted to rock, but every movement felt like my skin was ripping apart.

"Like hell I'm not going back there," Alex growled, and sounds of fighting ensued.

Roman glanced around, trying to figure out what was wrong with me. "Veronica, what happened?"

I inhaled deeply, ready to explain everything, but I could only utter one word. "*Alex.*"

The shifter lowered his head and scratched the back of his neck. "Dammit. I can't."

"Under—" My voice cracked. "—stand." My heart raced, and each compression felt like rocket fuel exploding throughout me. This was it. I was dying. The shadow had finally done it. But why had it waited so damn long?

"Your heart is racing too fast. It's like it's going to explode." Roman stood and fisted his hand. "Hang on. I'll get him."

I couldn't believe my ears, but I wasn't sure I had much longer.

The jaguar ran from the room, and I heard him step outside. "Alex, get back here. Something is wrong with her."

"I'm the king. He's not allowed back there," Matthew barked.

Yet another pissing match. I was going to die alone in this room.

As if the shadow had heard my thoughts, it appeared, hovering over me.

Be careful what you wish for. I'd rather die alone than with this thing. It had killed me.

"We'll take care of him," Sterlyn said. "Go."

"If you don't stand down, you will all pay for this," Matthew threatened. "You too, Roman."

I hated that I was causing all this commotion again, but I needed Alex.

My vision darkened as Alex blurred through the doorway. His cool hand took mine.

"Veronica, no," Alex pleaded. "Don't leave me. What's wrong? I need to know so I can fix you."

There was no fixing this. *The shadow did it,* I thought I said to him.

Did you mean what you said earlier? Alex connected, but I couldn't respond.

Between my boiling skin and fading vision, I fell into darkness.

Something sharp pierced my neck, and my blood burned even hotter. The last thing I heard was Alex whisper, "I hope you did because I love you too much to lose you."

I felt the same way, but I feared it was too late. Hovering behind Alex, the shadow's shoulders shook with laughter...and my heart stopped.

ABOUT THE AUTHOR

Jen L. Grey is a *USA Today* Bestselling Author who writes Paranormal Romance, Urban Fantasy, and Fantasy genres.

Jen lives in Tennessee with her husband, two daughters, and two miniature Australian Shepherd. Before she began writing, she was an avid reader and enjoyed being involved in the indie community. Her love for books eventually led her to writing. For more information, please visit her website and sign up for her newsletter.

Check out my future projects and book signing events at my website.

www.jenlgrey.com

ALSO BY JEN L. GREY

Shadow City: Silver Wolf Trilogy

Broken Mate

Rising Darkness

Silver Moon

Shadow City: Royal Vampire Trilogy

Cursed Mate

Shadow Bitten

Demon Blood

Shadow City: Royal Vampire Trilogy

Ruined Mate

Shattered Curse

Fated Souls

The Hidden King Trilogy

Dragon Mate

Dragon Heir

Dragon Queen

The Wolf Born Trilogy

Hidden Mate

Blood Secrets

Awakened Magic

The Marked Wolf Trilogy

Moon Kissed

Chosen Wolf

Broken Curse

Wolf Moon Academy Trilogy

Shadow Mate

Blood Legacy

Rising Fate

The Royal Heir Trilogy

Wolves' Queen

Wolf Unleashed

Wolf's Claim

Bloodshed Academy Trilogy

Year One

Year Two

Year Three

The Half-Breed Prison Duology (Same World As Bloodshed Academy)

Hunted

Cursed

The Artifact Reaper Series

Reaper: The Beginning

Reaper of Earth

Reaper of Wings

Reaper of Flames

Reaper of Water

Stones of Amaria (Shared World)

Kingdom of Storms

Kingdom of Shadows

Kingdom of Ruins

Kingdom of Fire

The Pearson Prophecy

Dawning Ascent

Enlightened Ascent

Reigning Ascent

Stand Alones

Death's Angel

Rising Alpha

Made in the USA
Las Vegas, NV
19 June 2022